Anonymous

**The Master of Wingbourne**

A novel. Part 2

Anonymous

**The Master of Wingbourne**
*A novel. Part 2*

ISBN/EAN: 9783337051310

Printed in Europe, USA, Canada, Australia, Japan

Cover: Foto ©Andreas Hilbeck / pixelio.de

More available books at **www.hansebooks.com**

# THE MASTER OF WINGBOURNE.

A NOVEL.

IN TWO VOLUMES.

VOL. II.

London:

T. CAUTLEY NEWBY, PUBLISHER,

30, WELBECK STREET, CAVENDISH SQUARE.

1866.

# THE MASTER OF WINGBOURNE.

## CHAPTER I.

### TWO KINDS OF LOVE.

MR. CROWE, the lawyer whom Wyvil went by invitation to meet at Caernarvon, was delighted to see him, and introduce him to his family. He was somewhat surprised that his visit should not have been paid earlier in the autum, and remarked jestingly that he did not think Wingbourne would have proved so attractive.

"There was a very sad occurrence in the

earlier part of my stay there," answered
Antony.

" Ah! true, I forgot that.  I remember
reading of it in the newspapers.  Poor young
man—sad accident!  But if what I have
heard of him be true, he would not be felt by
the family a very great loss."

"Indeed, sir, you mistake," said Wyvil.
" Everyone was much grieved and shocked
at the occurrence; unless, indeed, it might
be . . . . "

" Might be whom ?" said Mr. Crowe, observing that he paused.

" I was going to say unless it might be the
next heir at law, but I believe I do him injustice, for  though they were  never great
friends he seemed to feel his death  very
properly."

" Indeed !" said Mr. Crowe, "but I fancied
your exception might have been Miss Carslope;
from what I can learn, it must have been a
fortunate riddance for her.  I beg your
pardon," he added, seeing that Wyvil's

colour rose. "My curiosity is very indiscreet.
We lawyers get into the habit of asking
questions, and forget they are not always in
good taste. There's a definition I met with,
once, of a gentleman, which says he is the
man who asks the fewest questions; and I am
afraid I come very far off that ideal."

Whatever might be her husband's faults in
that respect, Mrs. Crowe did not trouble her
new guest with any indiscreet curiosity. She
had heard long ago such an unfavourable
description of the family at Wingbourne that
she was well content their names should drop
altogether out of discussion, and though she
would have listened with complaisance if
Wyvil had been disposed to speak of them,
she strictly respected his silence. She was a
quiet good-natured woman, proud of her husband, proud of her three sons, who were each
of them steadily pursuing or preparing for
their professions, and proud of her daughters,
two amiable and accomplished girls, as
different from poor Florence as the faultless

hothouse camellia is to an untrained dog-rose in a June hedgerow.   Mrs. Crowe was always very gracious towards any friend her husband chose to invite, otherwise her opinion of Wyvil would have suffered from his preferring to remain so long in the Carslope's society instead of theirs; but now that he had come, she was disposed to retain him as a captive to her bow and spear, and consequently studied to make his visit to Caernarvon as pleasant as was possible.

"We are returning unfortunately to London in a week or two," she said.   " We like to be home a short while before Christmas, and though we travel with post horses, we take very easy day's journeys.   You will stop with us, I hope, all the time we remain here, though it is rather too late in the year for mountain excursions."

" Aye, aye, Mr. Wyvil will stop with us," said her husband.   " He cannot get off for less than a fortnight with us, when the promise dates as far back as July, and he shall

travel to London with us too, Bessie; the
carriage is large enough, or he may ride on
horseback, if he prefers it. Did you not say
you had had the present of a horse, Mr.
Wyvil ?"

Antony was desirous of asking Mr. Crowe's
opinion concerning the stability of the firm in
which his money was involved, and he took
an early opportunity of laying his correspondent's letter before him, and telling him all
the circumstances relating to it. To him, the
subject was fraught with extreme anxiet
His right to ask Florence to be his wife was
involved in the chance of his having a present
home to offer her, for his pride and his honour
alike revolted from asking for her affections,
when they would be dependent for subsistence
upon her own fortune, or the possible chances
of his future profession. He was certain that,
let the worst come to him that could, it would
make no difference in her regard for him,
supposing that regard to be already his, but
this cruel suspense completely prevented his

trying to win it.   He could not help wishing
once or twice that Ellerslie had forgotten to
restore the mislaid letter until after he had
had his explanation with  Florence ; if he
could but just have been assured of her love
for him, it would have been easier to wait.
It would be long indeed before he could win
at the bar a competence adequate to the one
he seemed likely to lose, but reputation might
be sooner acquired, and (since Wingbourne
was really large enough for two), Mr. Carslope
might think the rising fame of the young
barrister a compensation for his want of fortune.   Still, two or three years must elapse
before he could even enter on the field where
his laurels were to be won ; and his heart sank
within him as he thought of the whole breadth
of England lying between him and Florence
for so long, with Ellerslie, and perhaps many
another rival near her constantly.

Mr. Crowe  read  the  letter  and listened
attentively.  " It sounds ill," he said, " very
ill, and yet I must tell you I have the very

highest opinion of that firm. I don't think
them likely to fail. Their credit is good, and
there is solid capital at the bottom. They
might of course get involved in. any general
crisis, but the times are good, business steady,
and I think you may trust them. At all
events, you would only precipitate the evil by
trying to withdraw the money, and I counsel
you to remain passive. I believe they will
weather the storm, and if you do not hear of
the crash in a week or two I think you are
certainly safe. Will they send on your
letters?"

"Yes, I left my address with the steward,
and orders he was to forward anything," said
Wyvil, as with a lighter heart he thanked the
lawyer for his comfortable counsel; and as a
fortnight passed on without bringing the
dreaded news, he felt certain all was safe.
So buoyant did his spirits become that he felt
all impatience to see Florence again, and
retrieve his omission. He missed her presence
sorely in the elegant and amiable home circle

to which he was introduced. The Misses Crowe were well read, accomplished girls, and six months ago he would have been delighted to be their companion in mountain walks or boating excursions; but now his heart was elsewhere, and he was insensible to the charm of literary conversation, and drawing or musical execution. In all they did, he found his mind straying to the question how Florence would have acted on like occasions, and he missed every hour of the day her bright smile of sympathy, or the unconscious flattery of rapt attention to his remarks, which she paid. All was flat and spiritless to him without her, and he was busy with his plan for paying a flying visit to Wingbourne, on his way to London, almost to the exclusion of all other interests.

He had a good excuse for returning, in his horse, which, if he accompanied the Crowes on their slow journeying, he might as well ride himself to London, as leave him to the care of a groom. Their road led them

through Marchbury, where they were to sleep
for a night, and by using extra expedition on
the road, he might be able to arrive there half
a day in advance. Five minutes would be
enough to learn his fate in, from Florence's
lips, but the remaining time would be none
too long for settling their correspondence with
each other, and saying the numberless tender
things which his troubled forebodings on
their last parting had caused to leave un-
said.

He told Mr. Crowe that he was desirous of
seeing Mr. Carslope once again, before he
went to spend the winter in London; but
though Florence's name was not once mentioned, the worthy lawyer divined that some
more pressing interest was at work than the
desire of seeing his old friend or even of re-
claiming his horse, which might very well have
been sent to meet him at Marchbury; but he
forbore to comment upon it, except silently,

"Half a day; he might have taken a whole
one, poor lad. I remember how I and Bessie

used to feel, when I was kept at the office over hours, and could not run down to Chelsea to see her."

Antony arrived at Marchbury, with a lighter heart than when he had passed through it before, and cantered on to the village near Wingbourne. He dismounted at the gate of Mr. Joy's modest house, and telling him he had only come for a few hours, begged permission to employ his servant in sending a note before him to Wingbourne.

The letter, announcing his visit in half an hour's time, was written, and despatched by the man, who arrived at Wingbourne at an early hour of the afternoon succeeding the evening of the interview in the matted gallery. Mr. Carslope had retired to his own chamber and had there fallen asleep, and the housekeeper not liking to disturb him, carried it to her young mistress. Florence, exhausted by her misery, and the sleepless night of weeping which had followed her return to consciousness, had not yet left her room.

A quarter of an hour afterwards, Ellerslie, in passing by the end of the corridor, saw Mrs. Williams leave the room.

"Is your mistress better?" he asked. "Is Miss Carslope up?"

"Certainly, sir; she could not lie still a minute longer, when she heard Mr. Wyvil would be here. She's dressed and ready to come down as soon as he comes."

Ellerslie's only comment was an impatient tap at the door.

"Florence, it is I, Ellerslie," he said. "Can you let me come in? I must speak with you."

"Come in," said her voice from within; and he entered.

She was seated at the table, Wyvil's letter lying before her, and her hand resting listlessly on it; her face was intensely pale and had that worn, sunken look which even one night of violent grief or illness will produce in a young frame; and Ellerslie involuntarily uttered an exclamation of concern as he saw how changed was her appearance within the last twenty-four hours.

Selfish as he was—as every act and word showed him fundamentally to be—he was not naturally cruel. The aspect of acute suffering, whether physical or mental, always awoke a corresponding thrill of pity in his heart; not listened to, indeed, if it was likely to interfere with his calculations and his policy, but sufficient to mar all his enjoyment in their success.

"I did not know you had been so ill," he said, anxiously.

"Was that all you wanted to say to me?" asked Florence, without raising her eyes from the letter.

"No, not that; but, Florence, you ought to have had the doctor sent for. You look like dying."

"I have wished I were, many times last night," said Florence, bitterly. "If it were not for my father, I would be glad to die, Ellerslie."

"Take care the woman does not hear us!"
said Ellerslie, hurriedly, and stepping to the
door he found Mrs. Williams in far too great
proximity to it to suit his notions of safety.
He despatched her sharply downstairs to her
work, and then returned to Florence, the
encounter with the housekeeper, slight as it
was, having removed the touch of contrition
he had felt on first seeing the poor girl.

"You have had a letter from Wyvil," he
said. "Let me look at it."

Florence hesitated, and drew the letter
nearer to her.

"I have a right to see it," he added, firmly,
though without any approach to harshness.

"You are asserting your rights early," said
Florence, but she lifted her hand from the
letter and gave it a slight push towards him.

Without lifting it, Ellerslie bent his head a
little forward, and glanced over it.

"Were you intending to see him?" he asked.

"Certainly, I was. It would seem strange
to him if I did not."

"I see no good in your doing so," said Ellerslie, speaking once more in the quiet, collected tone which was habitual to him. " Circumstances have put him on a different footing to - other friends.   In our treaty last night—you remember it, Florence—you have given yourself to me.   I am ready to keep my share of it and respect your father, but only on condition that you do your share— you understand me ?"

" Do I understand you ?" said Florence,— " I have wondered all night whether I did. Ellerslie, are you not deceiving me ?"

" Deceiving you ?   How could I ?"

" You would not, you could not—merciless as you are—have invented this to torture me, to get my promise from me," she continued, rapidly.   " Ellerslie, tell me what my father has done, or rather tell me on your word of honour, swear to me by all you hold sacred, by your mother's love—oh ! you don't re-member that, I've been told ;—if you did, you might not have been so hard upon me, a motherless girl; swear to me that you have not been deceiving me."

"I have not, Florence, when I told you there was a crime."

"Nor exaggerating it? As you answer me truly, you will have to answer here-after."

Ellerslie paused an instant before replying : not that he was doubtful of what he had to say, but his self-control had nearly deserted him. Her eyes, brimming with tears that would not yet fall, were fixed on his face with a pleading, questioning earnestness which well nigh overcame him. But another glance at Wyvil's letter steeled his resolution.

"I told you," he said, "that your father had done a crime which would, if known, deprive him of his house and land, reputation and honour. I am no lawyer, I cannot tell if after this lapse of time there would be further consequences ; but of this much, I am certain ; I have not deceived you, Florence,—were I willing to do so to win you, the truth is worse for your father than any lie I could have invented."

There was sincerity in his tone, and her last hope vanished.   She was silent.

" You know," continued Ellerslie, " that it lies with you to save him."

" Perfectly."

" And you are of the same mind to-day ?"

" Ellerslie, you are needlessly cruel !   I have given you my promise—I mean to keep it.   If it contents you to have me without heart or soul, be content ; but don't lay the alternative so often before me, lest I be tempted to revolt and choose my father's ruin rather than my own."

" To return then to Wyvil's letter," said Ellerslie.   " I can see only harm in your meeting him.   Let me see him for you.   I will tell him you are ill, and your father out or occupied.   He will learn of our engagement better from me."

" Oh, not from you !" exclaimed Florence, in uncontrollable grief ; " not from you, who

are the successful one. He must learn it
from me who have suffered equally. Ellerslie,
I must see him—it will only be this once in
our lives. You said he would forget me, but
I know he loves me now, and I love him,
and shall not forget—not while I have life!"

" You told me I was cruel," said Ellerslie,
with some emotion. " Do you think that to tell
me I shall never win your heart, gives me
pleasure? I cannot forbid you seeing him,
Florence, but I strongly counsel you not. It
will give pain to each. You could not tell
him of our engagement without giving him
the reason for it; and that, for your father's
sake, you ought not to do. If you will not
trust to me to dismiss him, write him a note,
and I will give it him with but a word of
explanation."

" Well, I will write," said Florence, drooping her face into her hands.

Ellerslie saw the tears trickling through
the fingers, and afraid of once more losing
his self-possession, hastened from the room.

# CHAPTER II.

## A GOOD HAND.

LEFT to herself, Florence tried to frame her letter, but her sobs choked her, and when she took her desk and essayed to write, her tears blistered the paper before her. She could not write those cruel words of parting, guessing as she did the object of his return, and the hopes with which he had come back. His parting three weeks ago had been hurried, overclouded, she fancied with anxiety; but still if he felt no more than friendship for them all, it was complete. But his last words to her at the hall door had meant more than friendship, and she had comforted herself with them through the miseries of the last three weeks; and she knew he was now coming to repeat them, and to make them perfect where they had broken off.

"Oh, what shall I say to him? what can I say?" she sobbed. "When he has been gone only such a short time, to tell him that I must be another's wife; that I have freely chosen to forsake him. What will he think me? faithless, falsehearted, incapable of true love, unworthy of his love. I dare not tell him what it is that has forced me to accept Ellerslie. It would be betraying my father. I cannot tell Antony that my father has been guilty of crime. I cannot let Antony hate and despise him. It is better he should only despise me. What will he think? What will he say of me? Oh! it does not matter as we are never to meet again; but how this cruel, cruel letter will grieve him, worse, far worse than if I saw him myself."

She fancied herself in his position, receiving such a letter; and thought that to her it would be less agony to hear of the separation from the lips of the beloved one, than to read it in those cold, cruel, staring lines. Letters were always more cruel than words. She might soften the sharpness of the blow by seeing him and telling him herself. She might extenuate her conduct without criminating her father, and though she repeated to herself that it mattered little what he thought of her, as they must part for ever, she could not endure that he should think she had given him up willingly. She must ask his forgiveness, and more than all, since they were never to meet again in the course of their lives, she must see him to bid him farewell.

She started up, though her trembling limbs were hardly able to support her, for time was pressing and Ellerslie would be back for her letter, and drawing a cloak round her shoulders and over her head, she stole breathlessly down the stairs and out by the front door. She took her station aside of the gate through which he must come from the village, and there waited, dreading lest Ellerslie should be on the watch, too, see her, and compel her to return.

She had not stood in expectation five minutes before the latch was raised, the gate pushed open, and Wyvil came in. He did not observe her and was walking onwards, when she put out her hand.

"I am here," she whispered. "Hush! don't speak. He will hear us. Come with me to the garden; I want to speak to you."

His exclamation of joy and gratitude thus checked, he followed her as she glided noiselessly through the groups of stable buildings, choosing the path the most remote from the house, till they reached the damp, forlorn garden.

Here she stopped in the nearest arbour, for her faltering steps could take her no further; and sinking down on the rough seat, she waited for him to speak. Her cloak was still drawn round her face, and he had no opportunity of seeing its extreme pallor.

"Florence, this is indeed kind!" he exclaimed; "more, far more than I deserved from the manner I left you. The remembrance of our leave taking has kept by me ever since, and it was to see you, and you alone, that I came here to-day."

She held up her hand to implore silence, and said falteringly,

"I know what you were going to say, Antony; but do not say it now, if you have any mercy for me."

Wyvil gazed at her in stupefaction.

"I am aware," she continued, breathlessly, "that I ought not to assume you loved me before you told me of it; but I am certain of it, and the few minutes that are all that we must pass together do not admit of delay."

As she spoke more and more eagerly, she pushed back the cloak which had hitherto concealed her face, and he could not repress his grief and concern at the difference the last three weeks had wrought in her. He had last beheld her full of beauty and health; he saw her now, pale, worn-looking, almost as if she had passed through severe illness.

"Florence! my own Florence, my darling!" he exclaimed. "What has happened? What terrible thing that I don't know? Is your father—?"

"Quite well—we are all well. There is nothing the matter except—oh, I can not tell you! but you must never come here again."

"I will not believe that," said Antony, kneeling down on the ground beside her, and taking her hand in his. "I have a right now to tell you how I love you. Yes, indeed I have; your father himself gave me permission. If I had not been a blockhead and absurdly alarmed, I should have told you this long ago. Will you not believe me, Florence, and think that nothing but an idea of duty has kept me silent till now?"

" And duty must keep you silent always," said Florence, a sob almost strangling her voice, " for I can never be yours.  Since you went, Antony, I have given my promise elsewhere."

" To Ellerslie? oh! say it is not to Ellerslie," cried Wyvil, springing to his feet. " Curses on the villain! he shall pay me dearly for it."

Florence gave a faint shriek, and caught his arm.

" Be still! you can do nothing against him. You will only make me more wretched. Antony, do not provoke him for my sake.  If you ever loved me, be calm!  Do not you, too, be cruel to me."

" I will be cruel in nothing," said Wyvil, turning round once more to her; " if you will unsay what you have said.  You are not engaged to another?  You have not done me such cruel wrong as to decide against me, without giving me the opportunity to plead my own cause?  Florence, say it was a mistake; it was a bitter one, but I'll forgive that. You have not, you cannot have given a promise to Ellerslie."

"It is too true—I wish I could say it was not," murmured Florence.

"You love him! No, no you do not love him," exclaimed Wyvil, passionately. "Whether you care for me or not (I would once have laid my life you did), you do not love Ellerslie. I have seen you shrink from him when he approached you—upbraid him when he quarrelled with your cousin—scorn him for his mean jealousy of him. I know you do not love him. What right have you to give yourself away to him when you are indifferent to him?—to break my heart, to violate all that is holy in love. Oh, Florence, think another minute—you cannot, if you stop to think, persist in this."

"I must, I must," said Florence, wringing her hands. "My father . . . ."

"Has your father commanded you to marry Ellerslie?" interrupted Wyvil, in a fury of

indignation. " It cannot be ! He would never
be so base, so false.    Florence, it is but three
weeks ago that I told him I loved you, and
he did not refuse me.    I received bad news
in a letter, or I should have spoken then.    He
cannot have betrayed me, or, if he has, no
duty, no reason forces you to obey him.    He
has once before tried to sacrifice you.    I will
not blame him so much for that.    Habit and
long affection made that fate less unnatural ;
but he cannot compel you to this.    No filial
duty binds you to obey him this time."

" It is not my father—you are mistaken.
He has no wish—he does not even know of
my engagement to Ellerslie.    It was done
myself—yes, done of my own free will."

" And you love him ?" said Wyvil, looking
at her in bewilderment.

She shuddered, and rose from the bench to
go.

" You do not," he exclaimed, triumphantly, and catching her in his arms, he pressed
her to him.    " You do not love him.    You

cannot look into my eyes and tell me that you love another."

Florence only clung to him and hid her face on his shoulder. The world seemed reeling around her, her heart beat as if it would burst its bounds in answer to his passionate appeal; but yet, her father!

"You don't care for him," he repeated; "your silence tells me you don't. You are mine, my own darling. Let me see you break yourself free from this horrible compact—send away Ellerslie. Let me protect you from him. Whilst we love each other, as we do, for your tears tell me you love me, nothing can have the power to separate us. This impious sacrifice must not, shall never be!"

"It both must and shall," said Florence, firmly, and she disengaged herself from his embrace, and stood pale and trembling, but very resolute. "Antony, I have given my promise, and I dare not retract. I cannot feign to you that I love Ellerslie; with this

promise given, it would be a sin in me to say
I loved anyone else. I can give you no explanation. You must perforce think hardly
of me; I cannot expect otherwise. I have
no right to ask you to trust me; only I must
exculpate my father—it is not his doing. Oh!
go now, we never must see each other again;
and God be with you, and with me too, for I
have no one on earth to look to for help."

She was going, but he held her fast, with
a loving, urgent force, that could not be
resisted.

"You cannot expect me to be satisfied with
this explanation. You know I cannot be. I
would trust you—I do trust that you will do
nothing wrong, but I must think that you
have fallen into some terrible error. You are
afraid of Ellerslie in some way, I am sure of
it. He has you in his power, and is using
it cruelly. Let me help you. I will go away
afterwards, if you bid me, and never claim any
reward, if you will let me help you, and know
that I leave you free and content. You must

grant me this. You cannot deny that Ellerslie is abusing some advantage he has gained over you."

" He is," said Florence, " and yet I dare not tell you what it is. No one can help me, Antony ; you must trust me when I say so."

" You are asking too much," said Wyvil, bitterly. " I would trust you—I do, in all, except in what relates to knowledge of the world. Ellerslie is capable of misleading you ; you are ignorant of how much he can do, or how little. In this, I may at least help you."

" Will you promise me, if I do tell you, it shall never go further—that you will keep the secret inviolable ?" said Florence, under her breath.

" If, as I believe, it concerns your father, you know I would never wish to do him an injury," said Wyvil.

" I will trust you then." (She glanced round fearfully as she spoke). " Ellerslie knows some terrible secret of my father's, which he swore he would betray unless I promised to marry him. He says his safety and honour depend only on his silence."

"I thought as much," interrupted Antony, wrathfully. "I know he was compelling you to it, through fear. Well, what is the secret?"

"He did not tell me; he said there was no good in talking about it; indeed, I don't want to know," said Florence. "It is something he did many years ago. And now, Antony, you know all, and you must go."

"And Ellerslie tried to persuade you into this!" cried Wyvil, more furious than before. "Do not you see that he is deceiving you with every word he says? He knows nothing against your father, else he would have told you the whole. He has trumped it up— he is trying to frighten you. Oh! Florence, it is our good angel which has made you trust in me."

"Are you so sure of that, Mr. Wyvil?"

said Ellerslie, who had crossed the soft turf in front of the arbour unheard, and now stood at his elbow. " You will make both Mr. and Miss Carslope suffer heavily if you try to convince them that my power is not real. Florence," he continued, addressing himself to her. " I advised you not to meet this gentleman. You have done unwisely in my opinion; at all events, the interview has lasted long enough. You had better go home now."

" Miss Carslope does not return to the house without my protection, sir," said Wyvil, firmly, and placing himself by Florence's side. " She has thought fit, as a friend, to confide in me, and I shall not leave her to your care. If Miss Carslope pleases, I will take her back to her father."

" Not till I have had a few words with you," said Ellerslie, interrupting Florence's murmured thanks, and drawing her arm, without ceremony, away from Wyvil's. " Stay here," he said, placing her once more on the seat, and wrapping her cloak sedulously round her to protect her from the chill blast that pierced through the leafless arbour. " Mr. Wyvil and I must have a few words of explanation, and I will come back then and fetch you."

" You are not going to . . . Antony, you have promised me you will not quarrel with him," she cried.

" I have," said Wyvil.  " Come, Mr. Ellerslie, this explanation is not unneeded."

" Follow me," said Ellerslie, and he led the way to the centre of the grass plot in sight but out of hearing of the arbour.  " You seemed to be of opinion," he continued, interrupting Wyvil, who was about to speak first, " that you could release Miss Carslope from her present engagement."

" I am," said the young man.  " I believe she has only entered into it from a misapprehension, and a belief that if she refuses, you have the power to injure her father.  I feel confident that such a power cannot exist, however much you may mislead her ignorance."

"You seem altogether in her confidence," said Ellerslie. "In this she has informed you correctly. I am sorry she has seen fit to consult you, contrary to my advice, but having done so, I must confirm what she says. I have become acquainted with a secret, which, if known, would be greatly to the prejudice of Mr. Carslope, and I have made it the condition of her acceptance."

"And you dare to acknowledge so base a villany!" cried Wyvil.

"I dare do everything, Mr. Wyvil, that will procure me Miss Carslope's hand," interrupted Ellerslie. "You think I ought to be ashamed of such a doubtfully moral procedure? So I might, were not the prize I shall win thereby, too great."

"And you expect to impose your falsehoods upon me also?" said Wyvil, contemptuously. "You have strangely mistaken me if you think I can become a party to this im-

posture. What proofs have I, since you decline mentioning the nature of the secret, that
one really exists, or that you have not invented the whole to gain her acquiescence?"

"Were I to give you proofs," said Ellerslie, "it would render the secret one no
longer. I am ready at any time to offer an
explanation; but it must be at Miss Carslope's wish. You cannot expect me to expose her father's reputation, when she is
making, what you seem to think an alarming
sacrifice, to preserve it. That it is a secret of
guilt you must not doubt. It is one I discovered seven years ago, and had never intended to divulge; but circumstances have
obliged me to make use of it."

"You have known it for seven years?" said
Wyvil, musingly. "What motive which has
kept you silent so long, can have failed you
now?" He met no answer. "It was, probably," he proceeded, "because disclosing it
could have brought you no advantage until
lately."

Ellerslie changed colour slightly. "You can make what inferences you choose, sir," he answered, haughtily. "I might reply, that not having till lately any views with regard to Miss Carslope, I did not care to use the power I had."

"There is something else," said Wyvil, paying but little heed to him. "There has been another change lately. You are now heir-at-law, instead of possessing only a remote claim. The secret you speak of, Mr. Ellerslie, is one connected with the Wingbourne estate."

"You may be right—I acknowledge nothing," replied Ellerslie, with cold reserve. "I spoke, however, of crime."

"And what authority have you to hide or conceal crime?" asked Wyvil, fiercely. "Who gave you the power to judge? If there is guilt, let it appear, or let the innocent be cleared. If there is crime, you share it by concealing it."

"Nature intended you for a lawyer, Mr. Wyvil," said Ellerslie, with an ironical smile.

"I may be doing wrong in not accusing Mr. Carslope. Unfortunately, I have his daughter's interests at heart. If you consider yourself justified in accusing him of a vague crime, and me of complicity, you are the master to do so. You may awake suspicions in other people's minds which could not easily be satisfied. Miss Carslope, by her imprudent confessions, has given you the power to do so; but I own I should be sorry for my relations' sake."

"Possibly," said Antony, studying his face attentively, to discover, if possible, some look of consciousness that would betray more than his calmly measured words; "you might be sorry, for their disgrace would be reflected on you."

"If, as you supposed, the matter was connected with the Wingbourne estate, I should reap the advantage as next heir," answered Ellerslie.

"That belongs to Miss Carslope, and not to her father."

"Come, Mr Wyvil," said Ellerslie, with

an affectation of indifference he was far from feeling, "you will gain nothing by cross-examining me. I am not inclined to confess to you what the secret is. It satisfies Miss Carslope; and as a friend to her father, you cannot wish to take any measures conducive to his ruin."

"That as may be," said Wyvil; "it is my first duty to consider Miss Carslope. While you persist in speaking enigmatically, you cannot be surprised that I rate your secret at very little. I shall go to Mr. Carslope, and inform him of the means you are using to compel his daughter to marry you. Even if he is somewhat in your power, his love for his daughter will make him consent to a pecuniary sacrifice. I will tell him . . . "

"Tell him all you know," interrupted Ellerslie, with an impatient gesture. "His reception of you will give you proof that I have foundation for all I say. Go to him!— I allow it—I desire it," he added, with in

creasing warmth. " Tell him what you suspect; and if you are not afraid of an old
man's anger, mention before him the name of
Susan Hoppner, and observe what he says.
There is crime, Mr. Wyvil—deeper than I
like to think of, or you to discover."

"Not murder, surely?" said Antony, in a
suppressed accent of horror.

Ellerslie vouchsafed him no reply, but
walked back towards the arbour, where they
had left Florence. She was still sitting
there, motionless as a statue, and nearly as
cold.

"I have been consulting with Mr. Wyvil,
Florence," said Ellerslie, as he took her hand
to help her to rise. " He has come over to
my opinion that the past had better remain
hidden, and that his interference could only
do harm. He will now say good-bye, and I
will take you in."

Florence raised her dark, sorrowful eyes
with a kind of mute appeal to Wyvil's face.
He exclaimed, hastily,

"I have come to no such decision. My promise of concealment was to you, Florence. I should dare him to do his worst. If you will consent, I have no doubt the whole may be made perfectly clear, without injury to your father or to you. Tell me only that you will trust me—that you will empower me to act for you, and you need no longer remain in the power of this cruel, calculating villain."

Florence had instinctively crept towards him, as if to seek his protection. He drew her arm within his own, once more, and went on defiantly, "We have resolved to try the issue, Mr. Ellerslie ; Florence has confidence in me. Do your worst."

"You may trust his advice, Florence, if you will," said Ellerslie, in an impressive tone ; "but you will have your father's curse upon you when he is dying in a workhouse."

The poor girl drew her hand away from Antony.

"That must never be," she murmured, in

a broken voice; " I cannot be his ruin.    Antony, to serve me, you must be silent—there is no other way.    I must save my father. Ellerslie has my promise; I shall keep it. You must never come back again.    You cannot help me.    We must say farewell."

" And you are content to let me go, Florence?" said Wyvil, reproachfully, taking her chill hand.

" Oh yes, quite content," she said, forcing a ghastly smile.

He dropped the hand, mechanically, and Ellerslie advancing, took possession of her, and led her to the house.

# CHAPTER III.

## NEW FRIENDS AND NEW PROSPECTS.

" You will hear from me again, rascal that you are!" said Wyvil, as he looked after the drooping form of poor Florence, and a pang of bitter hatred towards Ellerslie shot through his heart, mingled with anger at himself for his own inefficiency to help her, and idolizing love for her. He asked himself what was this secret which Ellerslie paraded so triumphantly. After a little reflection, he cast aside as groundless the horrible suspicion

which he had for a while entertained. Mr.
Carslope was not the sort of man who could
have committed murder. It was not exactly
from respect for him, that Wyvil came to
this conclusion. He could imagine him
capable of many another crime; but they
would be of the indolent, selfish cast—committed to save himself trouble or secure profit; but not hurried into by sudden passion
or fierce revenge. Ellerslie had probably
thrown out that suggestion, as well as the
name of the woman, to divert him from the
real scent. His mind reverted more strongly
than before to the belief that the secret did
concern the Wingbourne estate, and was of a
nature to invalidate Mr. Carslope's claim to
it, since Ellerslie had never cared to use it
when Godfrey and not himself would have
come in to enjoy the reversion.

He had no disposition to enter the house,
or to meet Mr. Carslope. He had no hope
of discovering the matter by applying to
him, for he was sure the instinct of self-

preservation was too strong in the Master of Wingbourne to welcome any investigation. He stayed only to have the hunter saddled, and left the place slowly and thoughtfully, taking the direction of the village, where he had left the hack on which he had ridden from Marchbury.

As he rode, he pondered still further over the possible nature of the secret. If it was of a sort to invalidate Mr. Carslope and his daughter's claim upon Wingbourne, its discovery would of course put Ellerslie in possession of the estate. Wyvil remembered to have heard that the former proprietor, the father of Mrs. Carslope and Mrs. Thurston, had divided his property by will between his daughters, the house and lands to the eldest and an equivalent in money to her sister. It was possible this had not been his last will, and that a subsequent document, reversing the decision, or possibly disinheriting his eldest daughter altogether, and leaving Wingbourne to the Thurstons or, in their default, to

Ellerslie, had been set aside by Mr. Carslope.
The concealment of a will came quite within
the scope of possibility; and if this could be
proved, Ellerslie might claim the property.
But this was no reason why Florence should
be compelled to marry him. Even supposing
Mr. Carslope had no other property to fall
back upon, which Ellerslie probably had as-
certained, Wyvil's own fortune was enough
for her and her father. Ellerslie might
threaten in vain a workhouse for Mr. Carslope,
if Florence were happily married, and had a
home of her own to offer her father. Never
did the prospect of wealth bestow more happiness, than his belief that his fortune was
still safe, did on Wyvil. It gave him the
power to free the woman he loved from a
tyranny she abhorred, secured her for himself,
and rescued her father from degradation and
misery; and last, and in his case so absorb-
ing was his love for her, it was least also, it
checkmated Ellerslie.

Arrived at the village, he resolved, while

the Marchbury horse was being re-saddled, to write a note to Florence imploring her to extract, if she could, the entire truth from Ellerslie, but to refrain from binding herself with any further promise till he should see her again. It was already dark, and he went into the little shop, which was also the humble post-office, to ask for a light to write his letter by.

As he wrote, the woman of the shop commenced turning uneasily over the contents of a shelf.

"Mr. Wyvil, sir," she said, "there's a letter come for you whilst you were away. I could not send it on to you because Mr. Nichols had mislaid your address, and I durst not send it up to be taken care of at Wingbourne lest harm should happen to it."

Wyvil took out his purse, and paid her the postage. A foreboding of evil crossed him as he received the letter in his hand, which increased to certainty when he saw the handwriting. It was the dreaded letter which he and Mr. Crowe had expected might be forwarded to him at Caernarvon, and on the non-receipt of which his late castles in the air had been erected.

He opened it; it contained the confirmation of his fears. The firm had failed and his entire property was swept away in it.

They were gloomy thoughts that accompanied Wyvil back to Marchbury. The whole structure of his plans was swept away at once. He had no hope now of rescuing Florence from the ruin which he believed threatened her and her father. If they were beggared through Ellerslie's means he could not offer them a home, or if a heavy lawsuit were necessary to establish their rights his purse could not be of any assistance to them. He felt confused with the suddenness of the shock. What advice could he now give Florence, except to yield to her fate? What alternative of accepting Ellerslie, could he offer her? If Wingbourne were not rightfully hers, but Ellerslie's, it would be the unkindest thing he could do to make her more dissatisfied than she already was with her destiny, for her destiny it must be, if poverty debarred him from coming to her rescue.

He longed to consult some competent authority upon the possible nature of the secret which had put the Carslope family into Ellerslie's power; but its uncertainty, its awful suggestion of possibilities, prevented his doing so. Even had he not given his promise to Florence to be silent, he might do her father and her greater injury by forcing Ellerslie to declare the truth, than by letting things remain as they were. Ellerslie had said that Mr. Carslope's friends should be the last to wish matters brought to an issue, and this was to a degree true; and it might be easier for Florence even to marry a man she feared and disliked, than to see her father brought to disgrace and ruin through her refusal.

Thus far he reasoned, as much as the

agitation of his spirits would allow him to
reason, during his return ride to Marchbury.
He could not think of Florence without
passionate regret, or of Ellerslie without
hatred and scorn, as a man who used an advantage he had unfairly gained, over a help-
less, friendless girl. That he could palliate
such tyranny to his conscience under the
name of love, made it worse to Wyvil's eyes,
for to its own cruelty it added the desecration
of what should be only another name for
self-devotion.

He reached Marchbury, and went to the
inn where he had been appointed to meet the
Crowes; they had not yet arrived, but he had
hardly been there an hour, before a letter was
handed to him by the waiter, who said that
one of the Wingbourne lads had brought it,
but had not waited for an answer. It was
but two lines—

" DEAR FRIEND,—Ellerslie has told me

everything. I am satisfied. For my sake
let no one know what you have heard; but
try to forget us as fast as possible.

"F. C."

The first few words were trembling, almost
illegible. After that came a stain of ink,
where the pen seemed to have been dropped,
then the hand became firmer, but less like
Florence's writing. Wyvil, however, could
not tell that she had broken down in the
midst of it, and that her hand had then been
guided. The letter gave him food for long
and mournful reflection, and was treasured
by him as the last relic he might have of his
lost love.

In due time Mr. Crowe and his family
arrived; they could not fail to be struck by
his dejected appearance, though for that night
he gave them no explanation. The next
morning, while the horses were being harnes-
sed, he seized the opportunity of finding his
friend alone to tell him of the disastrous

change in his affairs. Mr. Crowe was sincerely grieved, and his indignation at the imprudent, or as he declared it to be, fraudulent conduct of the heads of the firm, was to the full as strong as his concern for his young friend's loss.

" Scandalous mismanagement! worse than mismanagement," he exclaimed. " There must have been fraud. If there has, it will appear. I wonder what your father could have been thinking of to lodge his property in such unsafe hands; but they bore a very good name. I had a high opinion of them, myself. Might have been my case, except that as a professional man I've never accumulated much capital—I consider myself as my capital. It will be the same with you, Mr. Wyvil. Will your sister, Mrs. Harrison, suffer much from this? If I remember rightly the first letter you showed me said it might affect her, too."

" Never, with my consent," said Wyvil. " her husband is not a rich man, and her share was originally much smaller than mine."

" And it would not become a man to let a woman, who can't work for herself, poor thing, suffer a burden he can take on his own shoulders. I understand you and like you the better," said Mr. Crowe, warmly. "Is it a total loss? will anything be saved?"

" That remains to be seen," said Wyvil.

He thought possibly some trifle might be saved from the wreck, on which, with strict economy, he could live till he had obtained something by his profession.

" Then you must set to work with vigour," said the lawyer. " Hark! I hear the horses are ready. By-the-bye, I forgot to ask you after Carslope. You saw him yesterday?"

" He is well, I believe," said Antony, evasively. " I did not stay long at Wingbourne; this letter was waiting for me at the post-office."

Mr. Crowe took the first opportunity to inform his wife privately of Wyvil's losses, and

she, very prudently, began to doubt the advis-
ability of letting him still be of their party.

"It will cost him much more than if he
took a place at once in the London coach.
We travel very slowly, and put up at the
best inns; and his horse must be a great expense to him on the road."

"That's my affair," said Mr. Crowe, "as
I asked him to join us. You have got some
other reason, Bessie—out with it."

"No, for it's only for three or four days, and
much harm can't be done," said Mr. Crowe.
"The girls are very prudent."

"And, besides, to set you at your ease,
Bessie, he's thinking of some one else. Did
not you notice how anxious he was to visit
Wingbourne, and how perseveringly he
avoids speaking of Mr. Carslope's daughter?"

"Oh, you don't think it," cried Mrs. Crowe,
in accents of incredulity. "A girl brought
up in such a place." But she presently
added, "It must be so—he never would have
stopped at Wingbourne so long if there had

not been something of the sort. I wonder
what kind of young person she is. Well, it
takes a load off my mind. But will it go on,
do you think, dear, now that he's ruined?"

"I should not wonder if it does," said Mr.
Crowe. "I don't think, from all I've heard,
that Carslope is a close-fisted fellow, and
there's plenty of money on one side to make
up the deficiency on the other."

"Well, I had better let the girls know,"
said Mrs. Crowe.

"Ay, do, Bessie."

And it would not be doing justice to the
good lady not to add that, after this pre-
cautionary measure to save her own children
from danger, her manners towards Wyvil
were just as cordial as though he had still
been in easy circumstances. It was true she
felt uneasy again, when the evening before
they reached London, he mentioned, as if
casually, that Miss Carslope was on the point
of being engaged to the Mr. Ellerslie who
was the next heir to the estate. Mr. Crowe

whistled softly, and his wife, after a look of
motherly concern which she could not repress,
at the speaker, who tried to appear so unconscious, contented herself with inquiring
what sort of gentleman the future bridegroom
was.    Antony, restored to his equanimity by
her apparent absence of observation, was
able to return suitable replies, and the matter
was dropped, not to be again touched on.

Arrived in London, Wyvil commenced his
new studies.    They were unbrightened now
with the prospect he had hitherto held before
him, but he knew them to be his surest pre-
servative against unmanly despondency.    He
tried not to think of Florence, but this pitch
of philosophy he was not able to attain;—he
thought of her as he had last seen her, pale
and almost fainting with misery,—he pictured
her weeping silently in that large gloomy
attic, looking out wistfully at the scenery
which had been such a source of pleasure
to her, at the time she was in no need of consolation,—he thought of her as the wife of

Ellerslie, the hard, selfish man, who did not
care what hearts he trampled on if his object
were gained, and his face grew hot as he
thought of her loving, fearless nature, warped
and crushed by the blighting influence of so
unhappy a marriage. If he could, by con-
tracting any obligations or burdens for the
future, have been enabled to go to her aid, he
would have hurried to lay his fate once more
in her hands; but his poverty was an effectual
bar. He could not offer Florence a home,
and dared not by his counsels or interference
induce her to run the risk of forfeiting the
one she already had.

Ellerslie had not positively asserted the
secret to be connected with the forfeiture of
Wingbourne, and, though Florence had asserted
in her short letter that she knew the whole
truth, it was possible, either that her ignorance
of the world or of law might be still imposed
on, or that she might be solicitous to save her
father's reputation in some concern that had
nothing to do with the property. More than

once Wyvil began a letter to her, imploring her to have confidence in him, and tell him all she knew, but his courage failed him before he sent it: the letter, he feared, might fall into Mr. Carslope's or Ellerslie's hands, and her difficulties increased instead of lightened. On all these subjects he reasoned "in wandering mazes lost," but at no time did he ever imagine that she might become reconciled to her lot. He seemed to feel still the pressure of her head, as for a minute it had nestled against his shoulder,—the contact of her arms as she had clung to him seeking his protection,—and he could not imagine that a time might come when their mutual love would be forgotten, or when she would cease to hate and fear Ellerslie.

During all the time that his inner life was this chaos of bewildered doubts, his outward routine was commonplace enough. He read without intermission, hardly allowing himself time for the necessary relaxation of eating and sleeping ;—exercise he rarely took (his horse

which he would have found far too expensive
to keep, had been taken off his hands by Mr.
Crowe's eldest son), and he seldom allowed
himself any other relaxation. He had not
the time or the spirits to seek out his old
school-friends, though some of them were
settled in London, and Mr. Crowe's house was
the only one he ever visited. That good old
gentleman and his wife had been unremitting
in their kindness towards him ;—the former
aided him with his advice, and the lady, con-
fiding in the discretion of her daughters, and
also in Wyvil's preoccupied demeanour, gave
him a general invitation to her house, of
which he availed himself but rarely. A small
sum had been saved out of the wreck of his
property, enough to enable him to live
quietly and, as he had no debts, unembar-
rassed, and could he but have forgotten the
chief subject of his solicitude, he would have
been tolerably contented.

# CHAPTER IV.

## GAOLER AND PRISONER.

FLORENCE, on returning to the house, remained
for some time in conversation with Ellerslie
in the library, and when the note to Wyvil was
despatched, she went up to her own room and
locked herself in, and the housekeeper re-
ported that evening that her mistress had a
headache and desired they would not expect
her at dinner. Mr. Carslope, according to
custom, gave himself no further concern;
but Ellerslie could not conceal his uneasiness,

and proposed that a doctor should be sent for
from Marchbury.

"Don't you think Joy would do ? he's
always at hand, and Marchbury is so far off,"
said Mr. Carslope.

"Joy?" answered Ellerslie, with contempt.
"I'd call him in to your cattle with pleasure,
but for anything else, I am a better doctor
than he is. I'll ride over to Marchbury myself in the morning and bring Gillman."

"Eh! very well; I always liked Joy, but
I shan't mind consulting Gillman myself.
I'm getting weaker, Ellerslie, and duller; I
can't amuse myself as I used to do—I want
my friends about me, or something to talk
about. You're not as lively as you used to
be, Ellerslie; nor Flo' either, of late. I miss
Antony more than I should;—I wish you
had not advised me to send him away: he
might have given up the law and married
Flo' . . . . "

Ellerslie interrupted him.

"We shall be gayer shortly. I don't know

whether Florence has told you, Carslope, that she and I are engaged to be married."

"No, indeed! You and she? Ellerslie, you are joking;—you mean that you have asked her and she has refused."

"I should not be likely to joke on such a subject, Carslope. She gave me her consent only yesterday, but I would not delay longer in telling you what I know must afford you pleasure."

"Yes—ah! that's very true," said Mr. Carslope; "very great pleasure. It's odd, too, she should not have told me herself. And so, she has actually accepted you? I should not have believed it possible; she never seemed to like you particularly either. I'm more astonished than I can express."

"I see nothing so very strange in it," said Ellerslie, coldly.

"And when she has a property like Wingbourne in her own right!" pursued Mr. Carslope. He saw his guest's eyes flash, and hastily added, "It was her mother's, you know, Ellerslie; you can't deny the old man's right to do as he liked with his own. It does seem to me very odd! but, however, I shall be the gainer, for you will always stay here. You had better sell Llanfydd, you know. Still, it is very strange Florence should not have spoken to me of her intentions."

"Probably she hardly knew them herself, beforehand," said Ellerslie, "and to-day you have not once seen her."

"That's true. I am afraid she must be really unwell."

Then, with a sudden change of thought, he exclaimed,

"Ellerslie, you did not tell her I wanted it? You did not use my name to influence her?"

"I cannot be accountable for what influenced her," answered Ellerslie, colouring with some confusion. "I never told her you wished for the marriage. What she may have thought I cannot tell. I am sorry you think it so impossible I could have won her by myself."

"I have not said that—I should be sorry

to say that, Ellerslie, though I own I am surprised. I did not think she liked you. What did she say, exactly? What do you think can be her motive? Can you remember what you said to her?"

"Really, not exactly!" said Ellerslie, impatiently. "Next time I ask a woman to love me, I'll set you behind a door to listen. Come, Carslope, shall we have a game at billiards?"

"With much pleasure," said Mr. Carslope. "There's one good point about your marrying her, after all, Ellerslie. You will never have to return to Llanfydd."

This consideration seemed to comfort Mr. Carslope so much, that he passed a most tranquil evening, though the careless playing and preoccupied looks of his companion excited his remark ; but he consoled himself for Ellerslie's short answers, by repeating two or three times, with languid satisfaction,

"After all, I shall always have somebody with me, now."

But when Mr. Carslope had gone to his room, Ellerslie's anxiety would not suffer him to rest. Florence had seemed to him seriously ill, and in his heart he knew he was the cause of it. He longed for the night to pass, that he might summon the doctor from Marchbury, and though much alarmed, it hardly took him by surprise when, a little after midnight, Mrs. Williams came downstairs and begged him to send off at once, as in her opinion her mistress was becoming worse.

Distrusting the speed of any other messenger, Ellerslie saddled his own horse, and galloped off himself to Marchbury. Little did Wyvil suspect that it was the clatter of his hoofs on the paved High Street, which, in the dead of night, disturbed for a moment the silence of the sleeping inn, past which he rode. But notwithstanding his haste, the grey winter dawn was already breaking before the doctor arrived at Wingbourne, and when he came he pronounced poor Florence dangerously ill with fever. Mr. Carslope, when he heard

that her intellects were wandering, and that
she was in a state of high fever, and could not
speak collectedly, was much alarmed.

"She has never been ill since her childhood,
doctor," he exclaimed, piteously. "What can
be the cause of this?"

"Mental excitement probably, sir," answered the man of science, with judicial
vagueness. "Are you sure, sir, she has received no shock lately?"

"Some months ago, when her cousin died,
she was—we were all—very much affected,
doctor."

"Ah! it cannot be that—there's something
else not accounted for," said the physician,
shaking his head. "Keep up a good heart,
sir. She's young, and that's in her favour,
and your housekeeper is a good nurse. I
shall come early to-morrow and see how she
does. She may be better."

But in spite of good nursing and her youth,
poor Florence had received far too severe a
shock to recover as readily as the doctor gave

hopes she would, and his face lengthened every day, as for the next fortnight she lay between life and death. She was never wholly unconscious, or failed to recognise her father or the housekeeper, but she talked on in a low, rambling way to herself, quite regardless of their presence; sometimes, with an eager plaintiveness that went to their hearts, imploring them to save her—to take her away —to interfere in some way or other which to them was unintelligible. There was also another name she invoked, but this was not often when her father was by, and when he by chance heard it, he shook his head and sighed.

"Poor Antony! I daresay he often thinks of us," he said, "though he has not written. But it's odd she should be thinking of him now, for it's a month since he left us, and she never once has talked about him since."

"It's the fever, sir," interposed Mrs. Williams, and Mr. Carslope saw no further.

Satisfied that his child was in the best possible hands, he was, though very anxious, not disposed to disturb his ordinary routine of life in order to remain near her. The dinner table was required to be served as faultlessly, and he attended it as punctually as if his daughter were still there to sit opposite to him. He took his afternoon nap, and went to rest at night at his usual hour, without one exception, leaving orders with Mrs. Williams that if he could be of use in any way to send and wake him—an order the capable nurse never complied with.

Not so Ellerslie; by night nor by day could he be tranquil, and every hour, irrespective of the time of night, saw him in the passage leading to Florence's room, listening eagerly for the sounds and voices in the sick chamber, or tapping softly at the door to summon the housekeeper to give her report, till Mrs. Williams, who had a huge contempt for masculine intellects in cases of illness, not even excepting the doctor, became firmly convinced that Ellerslie, too, had a touch of the fever.

" Don't you, sir! don't you !" she would exclaim. " She's sleeping as quiet as a lamb now. She'll hear the loose board in the passage creak if you don't mind. If you could do her any good, Mr. Ellerslie, by walking round the house like a ghost instead of getting your natural rest, I'm sure I'd be thankful— but you can't, and you'd better go to sleep like my master, good gentleman! I'll let you know if she's worse, and if you ought to go for a doctor. It's all a man's good for," she added, as Ellerslie, satisfied that at least Florence was not worse, retreated, and building himself a huge fire in the drawing-room, the most central position in the house, and one where he could soonest hear if he were wanted, sat himself down to wait, till anxiety again impelled him to learn the last news from Mrs. Williams.

Had Florence's illness had any other cause than his own unkindness, his anxiety could not have been so great, but he knew full well that her dread of him, and her misery at what she had learned about her father, had solely brought on the attack, and that had it not been for his cruel love, she might have been as well as ever in her life. He tried to repeat his old casuistry that he had been forbearing long enough, that many another would, in his position, have claimed at once the rights the law allowed him, whereas he had been content to forego them, if only by so doing he could secure Florence. But this reasoning broke down before the doctor's next shake of the head ; and many times, while the fit of remorse was upon him, he was on the point of going to her, and telling her that he renounced his claim, and that she should be free without injury to her father. But the impossibility of removing Mrs. Williams from her charge, whilst their conversation lasted, and the dread that Florence's illness might be increased instead of removed at his sight, deterred him.

One day, while Florence was at the worst, his farm bailiff rode over from Llanfydd to report to him the state of affairs there.

" You're wanted there, Mr. Ellerslie. We lost four of the sheep three days ago in the deep snow, and nothing else seems going right at all. And Mrs. Evans has sent up from the Fell Cottage to say that her lodger, the woman Hoppner, has got a bad spell on again, and she's afraid she will die."

" Hush! speak lower," said Ellerslie, involuntarily. " She must not die," he muttered, " till Florence has kept her promise. Tell my cook at home," he continued to the foreman, " to send down to the Fell Cottage whatever wine she can find in the cellar."

" I did make bold to ask her, sir, but there was but one bottle left."

" I'll write you a note to a wine merchant in Marchbury," said Ellerslie. " It is impossible for me to leave Wingbourne at present."

The fever at length ran its course, and left

poor Florence prostrated with weakness, but, as the doctor declared, out of immediate danger. Ellerslie's spirits rose at the news in far greater proportion than her father's. All his thoughts of contrition departed, as he looked forward to a long future wherein he could make her amends for all she had suffered, and, when she was his wife, compensate to her for the cruel means he had used to gain her consent. His light-heartedness showed itself in his voice and step, as with newly-awakened energy he attended to the long-neglected business of the estate; as well as in the present of a ten-pound note to Mrs. Williams as an acknowledgement of the good nursing to which, in all probability, Florence owed her life.

"They tell me our young lady will be soon round now," said old Nichols to him, "and maybe we shall have the house as blithe as it used to be. It has been a sair time without her."

"Blither, I trust, as soon as Miss Carslope

has fairly recovered," said Ellerslie. "You will feel it like old times, Nichols, to have a Mrs. Ellerslie once again at Wingbourne."

"Is it to be so, sir?" said Nichols, his wrinkled face lighting up with pleasure. "It's the best news I've heard for many a year. I wish you joy, Mr. Ellerslie. She's a good lass and a bonny, and will make any man happy, forby her old father, who must have been sair put out at giving her up to a stranger."

Nichols lost no time in communicating his good news to the housekeeper. "And where have your eyes been then," she said, retaliating the scorn with which he had treated her on a former occasion, "to wait till to-day before you knew it? A child might have seen that Mr. Ellerslie meant to have her, all through this weary Christmas. I've had more trouble with him than with her father, twenty times running."

"Ay, aye," said Nichols, not to be disconcerted, "it's plain to be seen he loves her

like the apple of his eye.  He'll be a good
man to her.  It's nigh to thirty years since
the last Mrs. Ellerslie, her grandmother,
died."

"Well, God help her if she does marry
him, that's all," said the housekeeper, sighing.
"You talk of its being happy news, James
Nichols; you haven't stood by her bedside
hour after hour, bathing her poor face, and
heard her begging and praying to be taken
away and saved from him.  It's made my
heart ache many's the time.  And to see her
shudder and wring her hands, and make as if
she would fall on her knees, begging some one
to spare her, and to go away.  And then when
she grew a little quieter, she would look in
my face so pitifully, and say, 'I've not been
talking, have I, nurse?'  I could not find it
in my heart to tell her she had."

"It does not follow that she was afraid of
Mr. Ellerslie," said Nichols, "and if it was,
folks are not accountable for what they say
when they're out of their heads."

" And since she's come to her senses again,"
continued the housekeeper, " she'll lie and
watch for his step, and as soon as she hears
it—and she knows it at the other end of the
passage—she trembles like a leaf. I couldn't
help yesterday, before I went to the door to
speak to him, saying quite low to her, ' There's
no fear, my dear, you shan't have visitors to
trouble you till another month's over, if you
like,' and she pressed my hand and looked so
grateful with her poor pale face. Mr. Ellerslie's a civil man—it's not for me to say to the
contrary," she continued, pulling the bank-
note out of her pocket, and looking at it with
a gratified air, " but he'd have done better if
he and the old gentleman had let well
alone."

Florence did not recover so rapidly as the
doctor had given hopes she would. It was
some weeks longer before she left her room,
and when she did, it was with a step so
feeble and a cheek so hollow, that no one
else echoed her father's hopeful prophesy that

they should have her well as ever " before the snowdrops came." Indeed, it seemed as if, instead of progressing, she faded away daily. Her strength increased a little, as her dangerous illness was left longer behind her, but the blue circles beneath her eyes grew deeper, and her hands were " wan and transparent of hue." Mrs. Williams, whose panacea for convalescents was eating, plied her with trays of tempting food at all hours of the day. Old Nichols rummaged·in his cellar for long forgotten, cobwebbed bottles of wine to recruit her strength. Mr. Carslope proposed rides on her favourite horse, or even change of air; but she declined everything, or accepted it with such indifference that, in contrast to her former gaiety, it was worse than positive refusal. She neither read, nor wrote, nor talked, unless when directly appealed to, but leaned back, supported by cushions, in the large leathern arm chair, which her father had resigned for her use, and which was now drawn in front of the glowing fire, and seemed to take but little concern in what was going on around her.

Once only did a faint colour overspread her cheek. It was one day when Mr. Carslope said—

"I find, Ellerslie, that the hunter has been taken away. I've been out to-day in the stable-yard for the first time since Flo' was taken ill, and I hear that Wyvil came back and took him. Did you know of it?"

"Yes, I saw him. He only stopped a few minutes."

"And why was I not told of it?" said Mr. Carslope, testily. "Why was I left to think the lad had forgotten us all? It's more than two months ago. I ought to know what is going on in my own house, Ellerslie."

"So you would have done; but I was thinking of something else," answered Ellerslie. "It was just before Florence was taken ill."

His eyes sought her face. It was half averted from him, but what he did see was

faintly glowing; a second afterwards he saw
a tear fall on her hand, and he turned away
as if the sight had stung him.

It was long before Florence had the
strength or the inclination to visit her old
haunts in the house. It was a blusterous day
in early spring, when a few hardy flowers
were already peeping from beneath the light
covering of snow which had fallen during
the night, that she first opened the door
leading to the matted gallery. There was the
damp chill of *unusedness* in the air, and she
shivered in spite of the thick shawl she had
wrapped round her before venturing there.
Her progress was slow, for she was still
feeble, and before she had reached the library
she had twice stopped for rest. The room
was dark, but with trembling fingers she
undid the shutters and looked round on the
well-remembered shelves.

How long it seemed to her since she had
had been in that room. How far back, seem-
ingly on the verge of recollection, were the

happy hours she and Antony had spent there
the previous autumn. One of the volumes
he had sent to London for, to give to her, still
lay on the table; but she no longer felt
curiosity to open it. The happy light-hearted
self which she remembered in that room was
far removed from her present life—weary,
objectless, overshadowed by a terrible future
that was daily drawing nearer. Every hour
that increased her health, lessened the time
of her respite.

She left the library, the chill that was
creeping over her warning her not to stay
longer there. She mounted the staircase
wearily, and paused for a minute before the
gallery window which had witnessed the
scene of anguish between her and Ellerslie.
The place was little changed since she had
last seen it. The bare branches tossed before
it as wildly as ever, the wind howled as
mournfully, only a dull, sunless spring day
had replaced the struggling moonlight of that
December night. It was only herself who

felt grown so old—as if years had passed between this and that time. She left the window with a shudder, and opened the attic
door; another flight of stairs, and she was in
her old well-beloved sanctuary, where as a
child she had played. The little table was
still before the window, though spiders had
spun their webs over the panes, as if in emu-
lation of its sister windows. She cleared them
away and looked out at the vista of valley
and hillside.

Covered with snow, with here and there a
brown patch on the slope, where it had
melted; the dark stems of the trees dotted
irregularly over it, and at some distance the
leaden coloured river, gliding along between
its steep banks—it had still a certain beauty
in it. She had seen it from the same window
every winter during her life, but now she
looked at it with a strange feeling of dis-
union between herself and it. Beautiful or
dreary, she could never care for it again ; her
power of caring seemed gone, and everything

was alike indifferent to her. The objects she
had loved to look upon since infancy, the
kindly tones she remembered since she could
recall anything, the rough, loving faces—even
her father, who had been the centre of her
life, for whose sake she had sacrificed so
much, was almost indifferent to her. Her
heart seemed to her as numb as the chilling
air around her, only the dull, heavy weight of
grief which lay on it, or the sharper pang of
repulsion when Ellerslie approached her,
showed that it could still feel.

During her illness, Wyvil's memory had
been strong within her; but now that her own
fate was drawing nearer to its decision, she
would gladly have compounded for being
free, with the promise never to see him again.
And yet it was not quite so, for even then,
as she sat there at the table, and turned over
mechanically the leaves of a little writing
book which lay on it, her eye caught a slip
of paper, written over with small close characters, and her pulse throbbed wildly as she

caught it up. It was merely a list of garden seeds, which he had drawn up long ago, but she pressed it passionately to her lips, and falling on her knees, burst into an agony of tears.

A sensation that she was no longer alone came over her, and she looked up fearfully. She was right; Ellerslie was mournfully watching her. He had been there some minutes, though she was too deeply absorbed to hear his footsteps.

It was Ellerslie who spoke first.

" Florence, you are wrong to take such little care of yourself. You ought not to be here. Your father and I have been looking for you everywhere."

" I wanted to see the old places once again," said Florence, rising from her knees. " It may be long before I see them again. You need not stay for me, Ellerslie; I can come back by myself."

" Why will you not let me help you ?" he asked, reproachfully. " Why come away from

us all, and not let me be near you?   You
know that my chiefest happiness would be to
serve you.   Florence, shall I never make you
love me?"

"Have you gone the right way to work, do
you think, Ellerslie?"

"I would do anything—anything you bid
me," he exclaimed, vehemently.   "Anything
short of giving you up," he hastily added,
seeing her lips about to move.   "I will take
you where you like—to foreign countries if
you will, where you shall see something new
and strange every day; give you whatever
you can wish for, love you and serve you
with a devotion that any woman might be
glad of, if you will only let me think you are
happy."

"You will not give me what alone could
make me so, " said Florence, bitterly.
"Liberty."

"I cannot—no, I will not, if you prefer
that answer.   I gave you an alternative."

"It was such as I could never take, as I

dare not even think of, and that, you knew
before you proposed it," said Florence.
"Tell me one thing, Ellerslie.   If I were
to die, what would you do with my father?
he would be safe from you then, would he
not?"

"If you were to become my wife before
you died, he would be as sacred to me as if
he were my own father," replied Ellerslie.
"If not—but why do you talk so?   You are
better—you are not going to die."

Florence sighed.

"Do you remember the hawk Godfrey
gave me?" she said, as she carefully
smoothed the crumpled piece of paper, and
put it tenderly into the bosom of her dress.

"I remember hearing you say you released
it.   What of it?"

"Because it was dying.   I gave it clear
water twice a day, and every sort of food I
fancied could tempt it, and I hung its cage
in the bright sunshine in the yard, and then
in the dark passage, but it beat its wings

against the bars of the cage, and would not
take comfort, and I thought it would die, and
I could not bear it should lose its life for my
pleasure; so I took it out one day into the
garden and set open the cage door, and when
I came to look five minutes afterwards, it was
gone. I have often been glad since I did it,
though it was only a poor bird."

"And if I understand that parable aright,
you are fluttering and maiming your poor
wings against the wires, and look on me as a
cruel jailor," said Ellerslie. "It was pointedly
said, and well calculated to make me let you
go, were that possible; but it is not; my life
shall go first."

"Then," said Florence, calmly, "there will
be the same form of release for me, as I
thought was coming for my hawk if I had not
opened the door. Let us go down to my father
now, Ellerslie. It is, as you say, too cold to
stay here."

He locked the attic door behind them when
they had gone down the flight of stairs, put-

ting, as she noticed, the key into his pocket, lest she should be tempted to brave the cold there again. They were both silent till, when they had reached once more the warmer regions of the house, he said,

" And how soon will you resolve to trust yourself to me? When am I to call you by the name of wife, if I am never to feel the love of one?"

" It is a mockery to ask me the time. You know you can arrange it when you choose. I shall agree to it for the same reasons that 1 do now."

It was all the answer he could elicit, and she was too chilled and weary to be talked to more then.

" Was she going to die?" He asked himself the question, and dared not answer in the negative.

# CHAPTER V.

## FRESH ALLIES.

APRIL came, and half went, and Wyvil could no longer endure the absolute silence of his friends at Wingbourne. It was now five months since he had heard anything, and the suspense had become almost intolerable. He had long since sent his London address to Mr. Carslope, with a few lines expressive of his grateful recollection of his past kindness, and his hope that he might soon hear from him. Nothing had come of this; the letter might have been lost, or Mr. Carslope's mind might have been so prejudiced against him by Ellerslie's manœuvres, that he had no disposition to write. Antony waited, and counted the days and the weeks, making every allowance for Mr. Carslope's well-known dilatoriness, and at last, when no answer could by possibility be expected, he wrote again—this time, not to any inmate of Wingbourne, but to Mr. Joy.

His reply came in due course. " I could not, a short time ago, have told you much about the Carslopes," he wrote, " for I have hardly seen them this winter. The young lady has been ill, and her father has seen no company, and it is not my custom to go there uninvited; but three days since Mr. Ellerslie rode over and asked me to call. I found Mr. Carslope in worse health than I expected. I should say he is beginning to break up, though he wants seventeen years of the al-lotted term of man. He looks much older than when I last saw him, but he seemed cheerful and affable, as usual, and has asked me to go there again. His daughter—poor girl! is still ill; I do not think she will recover. She has no fresh attack of brain fever, but she is pale and thin, almost beyond recognition. Her father even, though naturally so hopeful, is alarmed about her, and hopes that a warmer climate may do her good, as possibly it may. Mr. Ellerslie proposes to go abroad with her after their marriage, which will take place in a little over a fortnight; it has been two or three times postponed on account of her health. We will hope for the best, but to my eye the journey will not save her—she seems dying. You will be glad to hear, though you did not particularly enquire after him, that Mr. Ellerslie is looking well, and . . ."

Antony threw down the letter. It had told him all, and more than all, he wanted to know. It had informed him that Florence was dying—from grief, doubtless, and that the loveless marriage was still to take place,

and she was to be dragged about from place
to place, an unresisting victim, till her
strength failed her and she came home to
die.

"Was this to be?" he thought, in his
almost maddened solitude. "Could no effort
of his break the spell? Was it unavoidable
that he should have gone away from her, and
left her to her fate, accepting without question her fiat that nothing could be done to
help her? Had he been justified in abandon-
ing her to her ignorance, her helplessness, her
loneliness?—for Mr. Carslope had neither
much sympathy or advice to give his daughter. What would have been the result if she
had refused to satisfy Ellerslie's demands?
He would have been driven to declare the
secret, accuse Mr. Carslope, deprive him of
the bulk of his property, and perhaps drive
him forth a houseless beggar. What if he
had? Florence would then have been free.
Poverty was better than bondage, and fancy
whispered that that poverty might have

united them instead of separating them. Was the loss of his fortune such an insurmountable objection? He had still a trifle left—£150 a-year; families, he had heard, could live on less, and he was ready to spend every drop in his veins, and every nerve of his brain for her support and comfort. There was no doubt of it, he had been too long inactive.

The first distinct resolve that arose from this chaos of thought was to go and consult Mr. Crowe on the best thing to be done. His promise to Florence had restrained him too long from seeking another's advice. The thought no sooner arose than he was hurrying down the street in search of the lawyer. It was the hour when Mr. Crowe would be in his office, and thither he proceeded, as fast as the jostling crowds that buzzed around him would permit.

Mr. Crowe was astonished out of his usual equanimity by Wyvil's statement. He tried hard to believe that the facts were exaggerated, and his suspicions unfounded, but the young man steadily persisted in his story, and at last, from the might of his earnestness, impressed a conviction of its truth on the unwilling ears of his auditor.

"I can hardly believe it of Mr. Ellerslie," said the lawyer. "I have heard of him, when I was in Wales, as a business-like, but, at the same time, liberal-minded man, and in no way likely to be so unscrupulous. Do you think it possible that the young lady was not so unwilling as she seemed to you? She might have been glad of an excuse to, we won't say break it off, since it seems you never had come to an explanation, but to . . ."

"Mr. Crowe! Sir, if this is your opinion of her, there is no need for my troubling you further," said Wyvil, hotly. "You do not know Florence Carslope, or you would not suggest such a possibility."

"Well, well, then we will take it all for granted," said the solicitor, smiling good-humouredly, "and Miss Carslope is exceed-

ingly unhappy, and sacrificing herself for her
father's sake. And now, what do you suspect is the secret?"

"I have sometimes doubted," said Wyvil,
"whether he has not invented the story to
frighten her."

Mr. Crowe rubbed his chin thoughtfully.
"Hardly likely," he said. "Ellerslie is far
too acute a man to commit himself so. There
were nine chances to ten that the young lady
would have consulted some competent authority, and he be forced to give all his
proofs. And now as to its nature—I cannot
think what scrape Carslope would be likely to
get into to give his heir-at-law this handle."

Wyvil mentioned the name of Susan
Hoppner, which Ellerslie had in his vehemence betrayed, and suggested that if there
had been any counterfeiting or concealing of
the will, she might have been a witness.

"It is possible," said Mr. Crowe. "If it
were so, she must have lived near Wingbourne, and her name may be known to the

servants.    You say there is an old man there
who remembers the former proprietor well?
He may recollect the name, Susan Hoppner.
So Ellerslie said that Carslope would be
startled at the name, did he?    It is a clue,
certainly, though a small one, and I don't
see how we are to use it.    Besides, I never
heard of his having any quarrel with his
father-in-law which would make it probable
that the old man disinherited them."

"When did you first become acquainted
with Mr. Carslope, sir?    Was it before he
married into the Ellerslie family?"

"Yes, I was with him when he first met
them, and I had known him two years before.    He was a young man, about thirty,
then.    I met him first at Liverpool, where I
had gone on business.    He had had some
dispute with a fellow passenger on board the
American packet, and wanted me to help to
settle it."

"Do I understand then that he has been in
America?" said Wyvil.

"Certainly; he had just returned. We managed the affair with a compromise. After that . . ."

"But stop one minute," interrupted Wyvil. "Mr. Carslope has assured me that he has never in all his life left England."

"He told you so?" said Mr. Crowe. "Why, what motive could he have? It's hardly likely. Think again. You mean that he has never mentioned his travels to you."

"No, sir, just as I say. We were talking, I forget on what subject, I think Mr. Ellerslie's journeys, and Mr. Carslope said expressly he thought travelling a waste of time, and he had never in his life gone further away than London. He has alluded to his dislike of travel more than once. I remember it distinctly."

"Umph!" said Mr. Crowe; "he could hardly have forgotten it—I believe he had been two years in America. That looks as if the suspicious circumstances which he has concealed, and Ellerslie discovered, had happened during that time, does it not?"

"In that case it cannot be connected with

the Ellerslie estate in the least degree," cried
Wyvil.

"And yet," said the lawyer, "upon reflection, it cannot have been done in America, for
no crime that Carslope would be likely to
commit in America, would render him liable
to the law in England ; as Ellerslie implied
he was—unless, indeed—"

Here Mr. Crowe paused, caressed his chin
again, and relapsed into silence.

"I am starting for Wingbourne this afternoon," said Antony, after waiting a few moments for him to resume speaking.

"Are you, indeed?" said Mr. Crowe, rous-
ing himself; "my dear young friend, that
must not be. Depend upon it, you would
only do mischief there. Depend upon it,
things had better be left as as they are. It's
best not to insist upon confidences amongst
friends. You will not be serving Miss Carslope—far from it, by making inquiries. I
have not the slightest doubt she is by this
time reconciled to her lot."

"Reconciled! I can only repeat, Mr.

Crowe, that you do not know Florence. I have heard to-day that she is dying—the prospect of marrying Ellerslie is killing her!"

" If she is really dying—" said Mr. Crowe; " but it is not likely. People don't die of such fanciful complaints as a broken heart in these days, my dear sir. I am perfectly serious, when I tell you, that Miss Carslope will not thank you for bringing to light facts dis. creditable to her father and consequently to herself."

" She may thank me or not as she will," said Antony, moving towards the door. " If she can be freed from her present bondage only by the full disclosure of the secret concerning her father, I will learn it, and make it known. I am grieved for Mr. Carslope if it be such as puts him within the grasp of the law, but I hope for the contrary, since it was probably committed in America."

" You came to me for advice, Wyvil."

" It is not my fault if I cannot take it, sir, I daresay you do judge for the best in com-

mon circumstances, but Florence is no common
character, and if by her means she could prevent a shadow of evil falling on her father,
she would sacrifice her life for it."

"Then think how she will doubly suffer
from any stain of—of guilt being thrown on
him."

"I trust it may prove to be venial," said
Wyvil; "but if not, I am equally resolved.
If she will authorise me to interfere, I will
soon force Ellerslie to make his accusation
openly and produce his proofs, if he has any."

Mr. Crowe looked annoyed.

"Well, well, how hasty all these young
men are," he exclaimed, impatiently. "Now
listen to what I propose, Wyvil. I will agree
to give this matter my best attention. I will
go to Wingbourne, question Ellerslie, and
judge for myself whether the young lady is
unhappy or not at her future prospects. I
will try to find out whether the secret is really
an important one for Carslope's interests, and
let you know the results."

"You will do this!" cried Wyvil, in a transport of gratitude. "My dear sir, how can I ever thank you sufficiently? This is more, far more, than I ever hoped for."

"I am not taking so much trouble as you think," said Mr. Crowe; "I have been wanting for some weeks to visit a friend in Manchester, and Wingbourne will not be so much out of my way. But I will only do this on one condition. You'll not thank me when you've heard my condition."

"It can be nothing I would not willingly consent to."

"You'll not like it, nevertheless," said Mr. Crowe, looking at him with an air of humourous satisfaction. "It is that you will leave the whole business to me, and stay in London quietly over your books, till I have investigated the whole."

Wyvil looked blank.

"I cannot do that—I cannot remain here when I might be of use to her. You must not ask me to do that, sir."

" On that condition and no other do I stir a foot," said his friend, positively. " Why, my dear sir, think what a commotion your appearance at Wingbourne would excite. If Ellerslie and Mr. Carslope are so much prejudiced against you as you imagine, you would not be allowed to see the young lady at all ; whereas I have really business that way, and can call in on Mr. Carslope on the pretext of old acquaintance. In fact, unless I go alone, I will not go at all."

Wyvil argued and pleaded in favour of his setting off also, but Mr. Crowe stood firm, and as his assistance was too valuable to be lightly refused, he gained his point. He declared that he had two or three persons waiting to consult him, promised to see Wyvil again before he went, and at last got rid of him.

" I've got into an awkward business," he soliloquised, when he was alone, " but fortunately I need persist · in it no longer than I like. I have provided for the young Quixote's staying in London. If he had abandoned his studies, and interfered in the matter, there is no knowing what might have come out. I can do as much or as little as I choose. For the girl's sake, I hope I may be mistaken ; but if it is as I fear, and she seems tolerably satisfied with Ellerslie, it will be best to leave it all as it is. Ellerslie has certainly behaved very unjustifiably, but it is very likely that if the poor girl is really dying he will not have the cruelty to push matters further, but will leave her free for the short time she lives, certain that the property will come to him at her death. I can point this out to him. At all events, Wingbourne is hardly off the direct road to Manchester, and by going alone I shall have the option of doing nothing at all if I think proper; in which case I shall not write to Wyvil until the marriage is well over."

When Antony returned, two days afterwards, from accompanying Mr. Crowe to the coach office, and otherwise agitating the moments of his departure, he found a carriage standing at the door which led to his rooms, and mounting the stairs hurriedly, he found, to his surprise, his door open. A soft rustling was heard inside, as if of some woman's presence, and through the half-open door the gleam of a grey silk dress might be seen flitting restlessly here and there. For one moment the wild idea came over him that it might be Florence, for what other woman could have an interest in coming there; the notion was preposterous, but possessed him, so that when he entered, and the strange visitor turned round, and disclosed to him the well-loved features of his sister, Mrs. Harrison, he embraced her with a feeling half of disappointment.

"Alice, dearest Alice, how is it that I see you in England?"

"Oh, Antony! I have but just come; and I'm so glad to see you," she cried, flinging her arms round his neck. "I have left Alie and Ritchie with nurse, at the hotel, and

came on here as soon as ever I could get
your address. You did not expect to see
me, did you?"

"No, indeed I did not. I can hardly believe that I do really see you. What has
made you come?"

"Alie was ill—so ill, poor child, that the
doctor said we must send her home at once;
and Edward knew nobody coming by that
ship, and I could not bear, so weak as she
was, to give her up to a stranger to take care
of, and the others were doing well, and baby
getting on nicely without me, so I thought I
would take a holiday, and bring her over."

"You must have been really anxious about
her."

"I was; and in another year or so,
Ritchie must have come. It is not as if we
had any relations here who would have
looked out a good school for them. As it is,
I must find a real motherly schoolmistress,
who will make them happy before I leave.
I might perhaps have trusted them for the

voyage to strangers, if we had anyone in England to send them to."

"I perceive, you count their unworthy uncle as nobody."

"Oh! it would have been very different, Antony, if you had had a home," said his sister. "How is it, dear, that you are no longer at Wingbourne? You seemed so settled there, in the last letter I had from you."

"That's all over now," said Wyvil, hurriedly. "But sit down and take off your bonnet, and have something to eat, Alice. I've only wine and biscuits here; but I can send for anything you like."

"So I find. I had a talk with your laundress, and I hear you live very comfortably here," and Mrs. Harrison took off her bonnet, and sat down at the table, and in two minutes diffused more comfort and home feeling through the room than Wyvil had been able to produce in all the months he had been there. "I was looking at your books and papers, when you came in; they

are in sad disorder," she said. "Antony, I
hardly expected to find you here, and
alone."

Wyvil was silent.

"I do so want to hear about Miss Carslope," she continued. "All you told me of
her has made me like her so much."

"Don't talk of her just now, Alice; I'll
tell you all by-and-bye," said her brother.
"Tell me now about yourself, and how you
left Edward."

Mrs. Harrison surveyed him anxiously; but
obeyed, and for ten minutes talked on without intermission, about her own affairs; then
she suddenly interrupted herself.

"And oh! that dreadful failure. Antony
dear, I quite forgot to speak about that.
Edward says it is absurd and wrong that we
should not take our share. I can't let you
be the only sufferer, indeed. It takes all you
have, does it not? When we first heard of
it, (it was just as I was coming off,) Edward
said the loss ought to be divided equally be-

tween us. I am sure your father would have wished it; it is but right."

"I'll not hear of it," said her brother, promptly. "It does me no harm—only gives me a motive for work, which does a man good; and you will want it when the children are growing up. It must not be thought of."

"I said I knew that was what you would say," said Mrs. Harrison, her eyes filling with tears; "but Antony, it seems wrong, and . . . . "

"I'll tell you how you can make it up to me," said Antony, all his reserve carried away before her sisterly sympathy. "If Florence Carslope and her father should ever want a home, you will give it them, for my sake, will you not, Alice?"

"Antony! what is it?" cried his sister. "Oh, what is the matter? How are they all at Wingbourne? Give her a home, indeed! She'll be welcome; but what makes you speak so? Is it all over between you? I expected to find her your wife already."

"She may never be my wife," he answered. "She is in the power of an unscrupulous, designing man, from whom I am trying to save her. I may not succeed; but if I do, it is possible that she and her father may prove destitute. You will help me, Alice, will you not, and let her stay with you till another home can be found? She has not a single woman friend in the world."

"Tell me what it is, Antony—what has happened to her, poor child, poor child?" and she listened with eager sympathy while he told the whole.

"And it is that commonplace, quarrelsome man, of whom you wrote to me, who is the cause of all the mischief!" she exclaimed. "And you don't exactly know what the secret is, which Mr. Ellerslie threatens you with?"

"He has told it to Florence," said Wyvil. "If she was satisfied, I had no power to force him to tell it to me."

"Oh, what blundering creatures men are!"

exclaimed Mrs. Harrison, with comic impatience,—"you haven't had one clear head amongst you all.    You have let this poor girl go on without any sympathy or help, because you did not like to interfere."

"Not that alone.    Listen one minute, dear Alice.    How was I to compel Ellerslie to be frank, if he gained Florence's acquiescence equally, and kept the honour of his family safe, by being silent?    And if I could have made him tell me all, it would have injured Mr. Carslope."

"Your being let into the secret would not have injured him," cried Mrs. Harrison. "Oh, I wish I had been there!    Florence never should have consented.    You could have made Ellerslie tell you.    You should have knocked him down, or turned him out of the house; in either case, he would have told everything to spite you.    If I had been there, I would have found some way; but you have let her break her heart, and perhaps be dying; and you say yourself she has no friends to consult, except her own selfish father, who would let her starve before he wanted a good dinner himself. How is she to know, poor child, what will disgrace her father? It may be nothing—it may be some insignificant boyish indiscretion, done years ago, on which Ellerslie has laid his hand. Oh! you have acted badly, all of you, and left her in the power of that bad, selfish villain!"

"What you say, Alice, seems true; and had I a home to offer her in her possible poverty—for it is Mr. Crowe's opinion, as well as mine, that the secret affects the Wingbourne property—I should not have delayed so long; but she and her father might have been deprived of everything, and I had no home to offer them."

"Well, have you any now?" asked Mrs. Harrison, with some sharpness; "and yet you have sent off Mr. Crowe, now, at the eleventh hour, to see what can be done for her. You have asked me to give her a home, and so I will, with pleasure, and take her off to India with me when I go back; but you could not have foreseen, when you dispatched Mr. Crowe on this business, that you would find me here on your return. Did you mean her and her father to starve, or to try how you could all struggle on, with a hundred and fifty pounds a-year, which is only a longer way of doing it?"

Antony coloured. Such had been his intention.

"Very good," said Mrs. Harrison; " I fancy Edward's proposal to make matters square will not meet such a contemptuous refusal a month hence, as it does just now. How I do wish I could have seen Mr. Crowe for a few minutes, before he went. He and I should have understood each other. I tell you, Antony, if he fails to make a compromise with that selfish wretch, I shall leave the children and the nurse here under your

care, and set off myself to Wingbourne.
We will see then what another woman can
do, and if I cannot be a match in duplicity
for Mr. Ellerslie himself."

# CHAPTER VI.

## MR. CROWE TRIES A REVOKE.

But Mr. Crowe, as he journeyed along in the smoothly rolling mail coach, had the very faintest intention of committing himself in the manner Antony believed and desired; and by the time he arrived at Wingbourne, he had fully determined that his visit should be nothing more than a call of ceremony, and a renewal of acquaintance with an old friend. He arrived towards the evening, and was met by Mr. Carslope, with the same exuberance of welcome which had once won Wyvil's heart. A Spaniard will, in his courteous language, place his house, himself, and his whole property at his visitor's "disposal;" and Mr. Carslope's notions of hospitality fell little short. Mr. Crowe was more than ever determined not to rake up anything to his disadvantage.

"You will see Flo' in the evening," said Mr. Carslope; "she never comes to dinner now with us. When the summer comes, I hope she'll be stronger; but she has not been fit for much since last December."

Mr. Crowe could not but be favourably impressed by Ellerslie's reception of him, which was as courteous as Mr. Carslope's, though lacking some of his geniality. This high opinion received a slight check, when, at the close of the meal, he had inquired if Mr. Carslope had not received, two months before, a letter from Antony Wyvil.

"I don't recollect, I'm sure," said the Master of Wingbourne. "Ellerslie manages

my correspondence. I have given up everything to him. Two months ago — yes, I
begin to remember. Ellerslie, can you recall
it?"

"Yes, and I gave it you. It was dated the
26th of February," answered Ellerslie, in a
business like tone.

"Yes, I remember it perfectly now. Was
it about anything special? Did you keep
it?"

"No. I never keep private correspondence.
It gave you his London address, and expressed
obligations to you for past kindness—nothing
more."

"You see how absent I am," said Mr.
Carslope, turning to his visitor, "of course I
ought to have answered it. Ellerslie, you
should have reminded me. Wyvil will not
take it amiss, I hope."

"I believe he has been very anxious," replied Mr. Crowe, and the subject dropped,
Ellerslie having acquitted himself of any
blame in the forgetfulness.

But when Mr. Crowe was introduced to
Florence—to the pale, dejected looking girl
who half rose from her seat and held out her
hand to him with a sort of wistful eagerness
when her father introduced him as " A friend
of Mr. Wyvil's, Flo';" when he saw the
languor of her attitude, and her sunken cheeks
and wasted hands, his heart was stirred with
pity within him.   Ellerslie seated himself by
her, and read to her for the rest of the evening, while Mr. Carslope talked to his visitor,
but the lawyer's attention often wandered to
that ill assorted pair on the other side of the
fire,—and noticed her averted face, her listless
fingers, and the indifference, mingled with
reluctance, with which she listened to the
reader.   He could not prevent his fancy
placing one of his own daughters in her position and wondering what his feelings as a
father would be.   It was too evident that she
was not reconciled to her lot, as he had hoped
to find her.   She was resigned because she
saw no hope of escape, but could he have

held out any such hope to her, without injury to her father, he felt sure that to the last she would have seized it.

Mr. Crowe was shown to his room, but there he lay awake, listening to the many noises in the house. A high wind rattled against the casements, bringing with it at times the sharp patter of rain. Tiles flew off the roof, horses neighed and stamped in the yard below, and inside the house the boards creaked oddly, and the mice behind the wainscot scampered, fought, and shrieked. To close his eyes was impossible, and he had plenty of time therefore to re-consider the situation.

He had fully made up his mind that the secret was no business of his, and he had a great dislike of entering into affairs for which he had not been retained. Moreover, Ellerslie did not look the man to have made his assertion with only light proof to back it, nor sufficiently generous to accept a compromise if he felt sure of obtaining the whole. Moreover too, the Carslopes, father and daughter, would not thank him for bringing a disgraceful family secret to light, especially if the rigour of the law were to deprive them of Wingbourne. There would be no thanks to him for intermeddling, and Mr. Crowe felt it would be the part of a wise man to keep clear of it.

But then there was that poor girl who was giving herself up, a victim, to shelter her father's name and fame. A very filial act, doubtless, and one that ought to procure her a blessing from heaven, but it seemed as if death was the only one in store for her. He thought of his own daughters and whether it might be their chance to marry men they did not love; he thought of a long departed sister of his, whose fate it had been to make an ill-assorted match, and who had died the year after, almost welcoming the release. He felt profound pity for her, and a wish that he could persuade Ellerslie to let her go free, on condition that the estate was assured to him. She would not to all appearance live long, and Mr. Crowe felt his eyes dim with an unwonted moisture as he thought of it.

But Ellerslie had inflexibility written in his face, and nothing that Wyvil had said of him belied that handwriting, and Mr. Crowe felt little hope of influencing him; but still he thought something might be done by appealing to her father. Mr. Crowe remembered of old the insouciance and carelessness of his character, but no instance of deliberate cruelty, and he thought it very probable that Mr. Carslope was ignorant of the force which his daughter was putting upon her inclinations for his sake. It was hardly likely that as a father he would permit it if his eyes were once thoroughly opened. He might be willing to make the sacrifice of his property to save her life; he might be able to open negotiations with Ellerslie, and at all events, and supposing the lawyer found him utterly selfish and callous to his child's suffering, the matter need be pushed no farther, and Florence's cause would only be where it now was.

Mr. Crowe fell asleep towards morning, before he had come to any decision what his future course should be.

It was not till a late hour that he breakfasted with Mr. Carslope, and Ellerslie had long since left the house on his usual tour of inspection round the farm. For some time the conversation reverted to the date of their former acquaintance, but at last Mr. Carslope said,

"What do you think of Flo'? I am very uneasy about her. You cannot tell, of course, not having seen her when she was well, but she is greatly changed. Ellerslie is going to take her abroad to Italy as soon as they are married, and I think it will be the best thing, but I shall be terribly lonely. I must have somebody to stay with me. Do you think Antony Wyvil would come? I would not ask him, only Flo' will be away, poor fellow. Do you think he will come?"

"I think he would lose valuable time in his profession by doing so," said Mr. Crowe,

" but Carslope, if you will allow me, as an old friend, to make an observation, I do not think your daughter is strong enough to marry yet."

" She's been very ill, that's true," said Mr. Carslope, " but Ellerslie will take care of her. He manages for us all, and does it very well, only it is a little dull at times. For some things, I felt more at home with Godfrey. But there is no use talking of past times, and Ellerslie will take capital care of Flo'."

" But are you sure, I am afraid I seem very rude, that your daughter's wishes point to this marriage as strongly as Mr. Ellerslie's do ?"

" If they don't, she need not have given her consent, that's all," said Mr. Carslope. " I had neither hand nor finger in it. It was no concern of mine. They settled it between themselves."

" You are quite certain you never told your daughter it would be very much to your taste if she married Mr. Ellerslie ? She might think she was anticipating your wishes. Girls are sometimes easily impressed."

"I never did. Candidly I never liked Ellerslie enough to wish him to have her. I do him injustice, perhaps, but my wishes, if I had any after poor Godfrey's death, were in favour of young Wyvil. He asked me for her also; did you know that? But I suppose she refused him, for he went away, and only came back afterwards for a few minutes without seeing any of us. But what is the meaning, Crowe, of this string of questions and insinuations?"

"Well, I think you ought to know," said his visitor. "I have been told by another person that Ellerslie quoted your authority to induce your daughter to give him her consent. It may be so, or not—there's no telling, but my informant said he persuaded her she was doing you a great service by accepting him."

"I never heard of this before," said Mr. Carslope, in amazement. "I must be a

strange sort of father to wish my daughter to
marry a man she does not like, to do me a
service."

" I am sincerely glad to hear you say so,
Carslope."

" Besides, I don't want to win the favour
of any man," pursued Mr. Carslope. " Will
you have a little brandy in your tea, Crowe?
You are not eating anything. I want no one
to do me a service. I should like to know
who your informant was."

Mr. Crowe hesitated. He was too close a
lawyer to give up his authorities lightly, but
there was such sincerity in Mr. Carslope's
indignation, that he began to think he might
settle the whole matter at once, and liberate
Florence by winning her father over to their
side. Mr. Carslope might even be able to prove
the whole secret was a delusion. The chance
was worth trying.

" I had it from young Wyvil," he said,
" and he heard it from your daughter's own
lips, the day he came back, which was after

she had consented to her engagement. Mr.
Ellerslie had persuaded her that he could do
you a great injury if she did not agree to be
his wife, and she has done so solely for your
sake."

"Ellerslie do me an injury! What can the
man be dreaming of?" exclaimed the Master
of Wingbourne. "And he has been deceiving
Flo'! she does not like him, then! I'll
make him give me an account; he will be
coming home in a few minutes, and I'll tax
him roundly with it, then. You have done
me a great service, Crowe; and I thank you.
I suppose the fellow thinks that because
Wallis is laid by, and he manages the estate,
I cannot do without him; but I'll prove to
him he's mistaken. Poor little Flo'! So this
is at the bottom of her sad looks. The
rascal! to impose upon her affectionate
heart," and the thought of his daughter's
wrongs caused Mr. Carslope to return to his
breakfast with renewed energy.

"He mentioned the name of a woman as

connected with the secret," said Mr. Crowe, anticipating the sweetness of triumph, " Susan Hoppner."

The knife and fork fell from Mr. Carslope's hands, as he stared at him with a face of blank dismay,—his complexion turned of an ashy grey colour.

"Susan Hoppner!" he repeated, huskily. "What of her?—what does Ellerslie say about her?"

"Here he is to answer for himself," said Mr. Crowe, in secret trepidation.

Ellerslie entered, and noticed the quivering face opposite to him,—the jaw fallen like that of a dying man, and the distended fingers.  He hastened towards him, demanding from Mr. Crowe an explanation.

The lawyer was about to give it, but Mr. Carslope interrupted him, saying, in a hollow tone,

"Oh! my God! Ellerslie, what do you know?—what have you been saying about me?"

"I? Nothing," said Ellerslie, looking bewildered, and, he added, thrown off his guard, "I have not betrayed you."

"I beg your pardon," said Mr. Crowe, who saw the matter was now past evasion. "It was from you that Wyvil heard the name of Susan Hoppner, and that you were master of a secret that would bring Mr. Carslope to ruin and disgrace."

"And if I said it, was it not under promise of secresy?" demanded Ellerslie, angrily; "and is it the part of a friend to blab it out?"

"No matter—no matter who knows it now," murmured Mr. Carslope. "How did you learn it, Ellerslie, when I thought it buried in my own bosom?"

"I have known it for years," retorted Ellerslie; "it was no wish of mine, but of your other friends, that it should be talked over."

"For years!" groaned Mr. Carslope; "and you have betrayed me!"

"I have not betrayed you. Come with me,

Mr. Crowe, and I will learn how much or how little you know."

"Oh! I am a ruined man," moaned the Master of Wingbourne,—"a lost and ruined man. My secret is no longer my own. Stay here, Crowe; you know enough already to condemn me. Let me hear it all over again— my disgrace and my daughter's. Oh! I wish she had died last winter sooner than hear this—I wish I had died myself before meeting Flora Ellerslie!"

"Come with me," said Ellerslie, sternly, to the lawyer, "I will hear how much you know. Not here!—not before him. What can you be thinking of? Come with me."

"Ellerslie! if he does not know all, don't betray me!" cried Mr. Carslope, imploringly; but Ellerslie paid no attention to his supplication, and, with Mr. Crowe, left the room.

## CHAPTER VII.

### TRUMPS.

ELLERSLIE did not apparently think himself safe from eavesdropping in the house, for he led the lawyer out into the surrounding yard, and round an angle of the wall, overlooked by no window save one on the floor above. Here he stopped, and the lawyer stopped likewise.

"Now, sir, will you tell me your motive for making this charge against my old friend?"

"The charge is one of your making,"

answered Mr. Crowe, coolly. "I merely repeat that Antony Wyvil heard you say that the name of Susan Hoppner is a terrible one to Mr. Carslope, and connected with the secret which you have repeatedly declared threatened his reputation."

"And what inferences do you draw therefrom?" asked Ellerslie, recovering his serenity.

"My inferences," said Mr. Crowe, "are—I speak in confidence—that this woman, Susan Hoppner, was privately married to him in America; at least such would be my inference if I credited your threat of depriving him of the Wingbourne property."

"It is perfectly correct," said Ellerslie; "Susan Hoppner was the first, the only real Mrs. Carslope. The marriage with Miss Ellerslie took place during her life, and was consequently void, and neither Mr. Carslope nor his daughter are entitled to inherit her property."

"Consequently," said Mr. Crowe, fixing his eye keenly upon him, "after Miss Ellerslie, generally known as Mrs. Carslope, died, the estate reverted to her sister."

" She was already dead," answered Ellerslie. " To her son, Godfrey Thurston."

" And not till his death could it by possibility revert to you. You have perfectly convinced me, Mr. Ellerslie, of your motive for keeping the secret so long, and now betraying it."

"I meant to convince you," said Ellerslie, defiantly, though in reality keenly sensitive to the tone of cool contempt in which the lawyer spoke. " Had it not been for your and Mr. Wyvil's persistency, the secret would have remained with me, and Miss Carslope, when my wife, need never have had any doubts thrown on the legitimacy of her birth."

" Have you any objection, sir, to tell me the particulars of Mr. Carslope's first marriage?" demanded the lawyer.

" Not in the least ; you may as well know the whole as you know so much. Susan Hoppner was a dressmaker living in Surrey ;

Mr. Carslope admired her, and, more honourable than a good many of his acquaintances would have been, married her.    Fearing the disapprobation of his friends, of his father especially, who was then alive, the marriage was concealed, and they started immediately for America, intending to live there till circumstances should make it advisable to acknowledge the marriage.    When there, Mr. Carslope became weary of his wife; her manners, tastes, and ideas were those of a class beneath him. He thought he had reason to complain of her—possibly he had.    He left her at last and returned to England, agreeing with her that he would allow her the sum of two hundred pounds per annum for her life."

" It was on his return that I met him," said the lawyer, as the speaker paused.

" So I understand.    He then became acquainted with the Ellerslie family, and fell in love with the eldest daughter.    At that time a report came to his ears that Susan Hoppner was dead. He was in some pecuniary embarrassment, and was indebted to the father of Miss Ellerslie.  Either this, or his attachment to the lady, made him believe the report without any inquiry as to its truth.  He proposed to Miss Ellerslie, and was accepted. Six months after his marriage, a letter arrived from Susan Hoppner to complain that her remittance had not been sent.  On the news of her death he had stopped it."

"As far as you have related the story," said Mr. Crowe, " our friend was more unfortunate than criminal."

"That is a distinction the law will hardly take notice of," said Ellerslie.  " Flora Ellerslie's marriage with him was not a legal one, and her estate therefore passes to her next of kin.  Her daughter, not being born in wedlock, cannot inherit it."

"And do you mean to insist on your advantage?" said the lawyer.

"Not as matters stand.  Florence has consented to be my wife, and it is very little to me if the world believes I receive my estate through her gift instead of my own right. And now, Mr. Crowe, having been so frank with you, I have some advice to offer you on behalf of our mutual friends. You have come here as Mr. Wyvil's ambassador, to endeavour to persuade Florence to break her engagements. You start—you would deny it if you could. Now I tell you plainly that if you succeed with her, I shall insist to the utmost of my rights, and that as Mr. Carslope has no property of his own, both father and daughter will be reduced to beggary."

"Mr. Carslope, sir, was in possession of a small fortune at the time of his marriage."

"He lost it afterwards by speculation. I assured myself of that before taking any steps."

"I trust," said Mr. Crowe, "that when you reflect calmly on the subject, you will be induced to accede to a compromise."

"Don't I look calm?" said Ellerslie. "Besides, I have already made a compromise. Till the last year it was my intention, if Godfrey Thurston died before I did, to have insisted on my rights, without any concession. Now I insist on nothing of the sort. I marry the lady, and the story of Susan Hoppner remains a dead secret."

"And if Miss Carslope resists, you are determined to carry your claim before the law?" said Mr. Crowe.

"I am."

"You must be conscious of the cruelty of your conduct. You are aware that, either in forcing Miss Carslope to marry you, or in depriving her entirely of the means of subsistence, you render your cousin most unhappy, and probably accelerate her death."

"Mr. Crowe, it does not become you, as a third party, and a stranger to interfere," interrupted Illerslie. "I have told you the whole candidly. I trust for the sake of my family you will keep our counsel. It will be the only course you can take consistent with your professions of friendship for Mr. Carslope. But if you trumpet the whole abroad, I warn you I shall not abate one jot of my pretensions."

"You are aware of the light in which your character will appear before the court," said Mr. Crowe, coolly. He was in full enjoyment of his self-possession, for the question was one of no particular moment to him—a keen encounter of wits, in which he was doing the best for his self-elected clients, but (save a good deal of honest indignation) of no personal interest. Ellerslie, on the contrary, was chafed almost beyond endurance. Each look and word of contempt from his antagonist stung him into passion, though he strove hard to maintain the same undaunted front as when he opened the discussion.

"If this matter comes before a court," continued Mr. Crowe, "you must expect your conduct to be very closely inquired into. Your frequent quarrels with young Thurston, who alone seems to have stood between you and Wingbourne, your attempts to drive him into evil courses, your concealment of the secret till his death, and unscrupulous use of it afterwards—these will tell strongly against you, Mr. Ellerslie. I do not say that they can destroy your title to the estate, but they will render your honourable enjoyment of it very doubtful."

" I am prepared for all you have hinted at," said Ellerslie, " and I do not deny that as far as my own feelings are concerned, I am very unwilling to carry the matter to its extremity. It will not be pleasant for me to proclaim that my cousin, Flora Ellerslie, was deceived all her life. But if Miss Carslope breaks her engagement, I am, though against my will, driven to take those measures."

" I have a proposition to make," said Mr. Crowe, more eagerly than at the outset he would have thought prudent. " Miss Carslope is, as you must have perceived, very ill. She is not likely to live long, and her father is fast failing. At her death you would naturally step into her property; it is but waiving your claim for a few more months.

If you allow the young lady to remain un-
molested during the short remainder of her
life, you will be no loser in the end. You
have already the entire management of the
property. Cease to endeavour to make the
poor girl your wife, and your object will be
as infallibly obtained as if you continued to
persecute her."

"Now you insult me more than by all you
have hitherto said," answered Ellerslie, becoming pale with anger. "Do you suppose
my only aim has been to secure possession of
Wingbourne, or that in loving Miss Carslope
I am thinking only of her property?"

"The word 'love' had better be left out of
the question in such a courtship as yours has
been, I imagine," said Mr. Crowe.

Ellerslie struggled again, this time success-
fully, for composure. "In the compromise
you have mentioned, all the concessions are
on my side," he said, after a moment's pause.
"What do you offer me on theirs?"

"A not too strict inquiry into your proofs,"

said Mr. Crowe. " Your evidence is defective,
my good sir. You have told a very well
connected story, but it is based on your
mere assertion. Where is the certificate of a
marriage between Susan Hoppner and Mr.
Carslope? How do you know that he went
to America for the purpose of concealment?
and, above all, what grounds have you for
asserting that the report of her death was not
true? You have not, I presume, the letter
dated six months later to produce."

" I have more than that," said Ellerslie,
quietly. " I have Susan Hoppner herself."

" Checkmated!" muttered Mr. Crowe, but
he would not betray any consciousness of his
defeat. " You must allow me to see and
speak with her," he said.

" You shall, to-morrow," said Ellerslie, " to-
night if you like. Excuse me one instant—"
and without waiting for Mr. Crowe's answer,
he darted away, and re-entered the house.

" The worst day's business I ever made,"
said the lawyer. " Foiled—check-mated

—routed at all points, and by that unscrupulous villain. He has got the law on
his side, and he knows it. I've one chance
left to work upon him. Susan Hoppner may
say something so condemnatory of his character that he would rather lose the lady than
continue the prosecution, in spite of his boast-
ing."

He was startled by voices above him at the
window, and looking up, saw it must have
been partially open during their conference.
It was Ellerslie's perception of this which
had occasioned his hasty retreat. He heard
a woman's voice saying passionately,

"He was not so wicked as you have made
me believe all this time. No one can blame
him much if the whole is known. Why did
you not tell me he believed he was free? No
real disgrace could come upon him for
having believed the report of her death."

"I said ruin as well as disgrace," said
Ellerslie, peremptorily. "Do not you think
it would break his heart to be expelled from

his home in his old age? Come away from the window, Florence. You were not meant to overhear us. Mr. Crowe is going away directly, and I am going away with him."

"You are going, too," she cried, with an accent of relief.

"Yes," said Ellerslie. "You will be rid of me for this one day at least. Florence, if I am killing you, as you say, you are revenging yourself well."

The window was closed, and Mr. Crowe heard no more. In half an hour more, he and Ellerslie were mounted, and on their way to the mountains. Ellerslie would not permit him to bid farewell to Mr. Carslope. "You can see him," he said, "on your return to-morrow, when you are fully satisfied," and Mr. Crowe, on learning from Nichols that his master seemed greatly indisposed, assented.

They passed the river over a new and substantially built stone bridge, to which the workmen were still putting the finishing

touches.    The lawyer saw his companion
glance involuntarily down the stream, and
inquired,

" Was it in this river your cousin met his
death ?"

" Yes, about here," answered Ellerslie, but
one of the workmen said,

" It was here, sure enough, sir, and off the
very bridge which stood where this does now.
No fear of this being carried away by the
water like the old one ;  for all that the river
looks very different after the rains to what it
does now, sir."

They rode on, Ellerslie talking indifferently
of other things ; it was equally his inclination
to avoid subjects of quarrel, as his pride to
show he was fearless of the result of Mr.
Crowe's investigations.

It had been their intention to have reached
the Fell Cottage that evening, but the lawyer
who had been long unused to the saddle,
found himself so stiff and tired by the time
they had gone two-thirds of the distance, that

Ellerslie proposed they should stay for the night at Llanfydd, and proceed the next morning.    Mr. Crowe gladly agreed, and they reached the solitary, unsheltered farmhouse, which looked all the more desolate now from its master's six months absence. Here they passed the evening, but when the lawyer was shown to his room, whose sloping roof and narrow dimensions contrasted with his last night's ampler accommodation at Wingbourne,—when the moon was " on the lake, and the mist on the brae,"—Ellerslie opened the hall door and stepped out upon the hill side.

A half formed idea was running in his mind to ride over himself to the Fell Cottage, and instruct the woman there in the story she should tell when they both visited her the next day, and he was walking to the stable, intending to saddle his horse himself and set off, when second thoughts checked his design.    He reflected that she could not, however much taken by surprise, say anything to

mar the truth of his story.    She could only
add fresh evidence, which Mr. Crowe was
anxious to obtain,  and which could only make
Ellerslie's cause the  stronger ; and she would,
in all probability,  tell  her  tale more simply,
for not being  forewarned.    It was of importance that Mr. Crowe should consider her evidence conclusive, and also that he should  not
imagine Ellerslie's dealings to be more crooked
than he did already.    Ellerslie therefore decided to let the visit take her unprepared ; it
would be the best for him in the end.

# CHAPTER VIII.

### CROSS QUESTIONING.

THE two gentlemen set off the next morning soon after sunrise, and it was still early
when they arrived at the Fell Cottage.    The
woman of the house hurried out on hearing
the horses, and seeing who they were, curt-
sied joyfully.

"The sight of you will do her a world of
good, Mr. Ellerslie ; poor thing, she's been
up and down in her mind thinking she was
dying, and not a soul but myself and my husband to talk to.    She did ask dreadfully to

see a doctor to be sure, but I did not like to
send for one without your orders, and before
I could send over to Llanfydd, the bad fit
was over for a while."

"I'll have a doctor come and see her without delay," said Ellerslie. "Meanwhile she
is better, is she not, Mrs. Evans? Is she able
to talk? I have brought this gentleman here
to speak to her."

"Able? oh, she's always able to talk,"
said Mrs. Evans. "Will you walk in, gentlemen, and take a seat in the kitchen, while I
run and tell her that gentlefolks are coming
to see her."

Mr. Crowe dismounted, and followed Ellerslie into the little kitchen, where the
children crowded together and stared at
them. Ellerslie, anxious to be alone, dis-
missed them with what seemed to them a
boundless present of sixpences, and a com-
mand to run out of doors and play, and then
he spoke to Mr. Crowe in a low voice, and
glancing often at the inner door.

" I want to satisfy you of my power to support my evidence, should the case ever come
to be tried.    You are about to see Mrs. Carslope, or Hoppner, as for prudence sake she
has been called ever since she came here.    I
have only therefore to tell you the name of
the village church where she was married, and
where you will still find the register ; I have
seen it myself, it is away in Surrey.    Next I
have the written attestation of the people
with whom she lived in America ever since
her husband abandoned her, and of the captain who received her from their hands and
brought her over.    These, which I procured
some years ago, are sufficient proofs of her
identity with the person she declares herself
to be."

" There is one thing you have forgotten,"
said Mr. Crowe.    " How can you be certain
that Mr. Carslope ever received the letter she
wrote six months after his second marriage."

" I do not see how that affects its ille-
gality."

" Not at all, but it does affect Mr. Carslope's character, to have it proved that at the time he believed her to be dead."

" True," said Ellerslie. " I grant I cannot prove that he ever believed she was. I have been content to infer it was so from a remaining respect for his character. As to the letter I have it, or part of it, in my possession."

" Indeed!" said Mr. Crowe, frowning. "You seemed to have carried your researches to the verge of discretion, Mr. Ellerslie. Since when has it been the custom of one gentleman to lay violent hands on the correspondence of another ?"

" When that other has usurped for years a property which is not his own, such a deed, if it were committed, would be excusable," said Ellerslie, haughtily; "but you judge too hastily, sir. I had that letter many years before I made use of it. It was in this manner. When I was a lad of twelve or thirteen, I was at Wingbourne. I had a fancy at that time for collecting stones, fossils, anything. One

day I brought a number of new specimens into the house.    I wanted paper to wrap them
in, and took amongst others the torn sheet of
a letter."

"And read it, then ?" asked Mr. Crowe.

"I glanced through it as I was wrapping
the stones up.    All the first part, together with
the name of the person to whom it was addressed, was torn away.    The letter itself was
in legal language—quite incomprehensible to
me; and the signature was Susan Carslope, a
person I had never heard of.    I forgot all
about it; the fossils were discarded for something else, and for a dozen years I never gave
a thought to the matter.    When I heard this
woman's story, some dim recollection came
over me of having seen her name before, and
I remembered where.    I went home and
searched for it, and after two or three days
looking, found it.    Mrs. Carslope tells me she
wrote, or had written for her, three times."

As Ellerslie finished his explanation, the

door of the inner room opened, and Mrs. Evans came out.

" She's ready now, sir; will you have the kindness to walk in ?"

They went in to the small, but scrupulously clean room. The woman they came to seek was lying in bed, propped up with pillows. She was worn and thin with long illness, but there were no marks of want in her appearance, and everything around her room wore rather the comfortable aspect of a well-ordered farmer's house, than of a cottage so poorly furnished in its other apartments. Her face must have once been handsome, and her hands were small, and from long rest from work white and smooth. On one finger Mr. Crowe noticed the sparkle of her wedding ring.

She looked bright and cheerful on seeing Ellerslie.

" You've come at last, sir—that's very good of you. Not before you were wanted, I'm

sure, for I've looked out for you day after day
and wondered when you would be here.   It's
a shame of me to ask you to come, when you
have so much to do, and I can be of no
use."

"I have brought this gentleman, Mrs.
Hoppner, who wishes to ask some questions
about your history, and you will be doing me
a real service if you will tell him everything
he wants to know."

"I must be allowed, sir, to question her
myself, and alone," said Mr. Crowe. "I hope
you have no objection."

"None at all," said Ellerslie, without hesitation.  "Mrs. Hoppner, you may talk to him
as freely as you would to myself."

"And are you going, sir?  I'd a hundred
things to say to you."

"I will come back before we leave," answered Ellerslie, and he left the lawyer alone
with her.

The woman looked at him rather apprehensively, and her fingers clutched nervously at a large roll of knitting that lay on the bed. She waited for the lawyer to begin to question her, which he did presently.

"Is it long since you have known Mr. Ellerslie?"

"It will be eight years come next October," she replied. "Eight years since I've been a weary weight on his hands. I had but just come to England in the August before."

"Did you go to him because he was a relative of the—the family?"

"No, sir, he came to me; I'd never heard of him, I'd hardly heard their names. I left America in order to find the gentleman, my husband, out. You know everything perhaps already, sir?"

"Yes," said Mr. Crowe, "all that Mr. Ellerslie could tell me. Your marriage with Mr. Carslope and his desertion of you afterwards. Go on now with your own story. You wrote to him, or got a lawyer to write for you, did you?"

" Yes, sir, as soon as the money he promised to pay me did not come. I'd had one
half-year's money, and then I was taken ill
with fever, and the doctor and one thing and
another used it all up. Three other people in
the house died, and I was nigh unto death's
door. I wrote when I grew better, to the
address he used to be at when I first met him
—his grand club house in London—but I had
no answer and no money came; and by-and-
bye I wrote again, but still not a word. I
took in work then, and when that did not do,
tried to get a place, and did one thing and
another just as I could turn my hand to it,
and get people to trust me. I used to fancy
sometimes that he must be dead, for he never
could have forgotten me so ; and then again
I felt all on fire, because he had taken me to
a strange country, and left me to manage for
myself. I wanted to have revenge on him,
and yet, when I thought he was dead, I felt
so unhappy."

"But why did you delay so long in returning to England?" asked the lawyer.

"Oh, sir, money was wanting—one thing
and another. I used to drink, more's the
pity, whenever I got the chance; it was a
habit I got into when I was first in trouble,
and through that I lost my customers, and the
money I had saved was spent whilst looking
out again. I had much ado to live, let alone
getting my passage money. At last I scraped
it together; the captain was a friend to the
people where I lodged, and did not charge
me the full price, and I came over. I asked
about Mr. Carslope in Liverpool, and after
much going here and there, and worrying,
for I did not know the right persons to ask, I
heard he was alive and married. The man
who told me did not know that his wife was
already dead. Then I thought I'd go to him
and make him do something for me. I did
not want to injure the lady, but I was his
real wife and no one else; and I felt bitter

against him for leaving me so long to want."

" Did you then write to him again ?"

" No, sir, I set out on foot and walked, and begged my way, for I had no money left. One evening I found I had mistaken my road, when I stopped to ask my way at a public-house. I was terribly tired, and I begged for a glass, and the landlord gave me some, more than was good for me, for I'd gone without some time, and my head could not stand it. I set off again, and in the dark I fell over the quarry."

" The quarry ! and that has lamed you ever since ?"

" Lamed me, sir? indeed you may say so. I've been bedridden for seven years and a half," said the woman. " It was an old quarry, and there was no one there, and I lay and groaned through that night and the next day, and when at last, as the sun went down, I heard a voice from the top call out, ' Is any

one there? Any one hurt?' it sounded the
sweetest music I ever heard. I called out as
loudly as I could, which was not much, for
my voice was almost gone, and he left his
horse and came down by a roundabout path,
and lifted me up in his arms, and carried me
as gently as he could to the top of the quarry.
If I'd been his own mother he could not have
been more careful or kind. There is not a
gentleman in England who can match him for
a good heart."

"No man could have done less than come
to your assistance," said Mr. Crowe.

"Many a man would have done less than
he has for me, sir. He brought me here to
this house, and here I've been ever since, and
he's paid for my room and nursing for these
eight years, and not meanly, so that Mrs.
Evans might be glad for me to die, and rid
her of the trouble, or as if I was in the workhouse, but like a gentlewoman. He has sent
me down wine from his house, and spared his

own cook now and then to show Mrs. Evans
how to do for the sick, and he's come to see
me when I was worse than usual ; and all that
for an utter stranger, sir.    There isn't a
creature on this earth that Mr. Ellerslie could
be unkind to."

The lawyer smiled to hear her eulogium,
and then sighed to think how it had been
proved false in the case of poor Florence.

" He had his own reasons for keeping you
alive and devoted to him, as a witness against
your husband," he said.

" He knew nothing about my history for
many a month," persisted the invalid.    " It
was only when I saw I should never be up
again, and that he was a real friend, and
would perhaps manage for me, that I told him.
He was surprised enough to hear it.    I was
bent upon making Mr. Carslope acknowledge
me, but Mr. Ellerslie would not hear of it.
He told me his wife was now dead, but that
if I came forward, it would make Mr. Car-

slope lose all the property he now had, and that I should get nothing by it but my revenge, for that Mr. Carslope could do nothing for me. He said a time might come when my evidence would be wanted, and he begged me to wait till then. Well, sir, he talked to me so Christian-like, and promised me, if I'd keep silence, he'd take care of me, that I told him I would, and I've never breathed a word of it to any living soul except to him, till he brought you here to see me."

"And I hope you never will, Mrs. Hoppner," said the lawyer.

"That's as may be, sir. I'll do nothing against Mr. Ellerslie's advice; but if he wants me to tell, I'm ready to do it, for he's been the best and only friend I've had for many a long year."

# CHAPTER IX.

## THE BIRD FLUTTERS.

MR. CROWE returned to Wingbourne after a long cross-examination, sorely discouraged and perplexed. He was conscious that he had, with the best intentions, played a sorry part. He had interfered, in what must always seem an unwarrantable manner, in his old acquaintance's concerns, and had achieved no good results therefrom. He had not been able to defeat Ellerslie's manœuvres, or to liberate Florence, and he had, in addition, overwhelmed Mr. Carslope with the humiliating consciousness that his crime and disgrace were known, even beyond his own family. This was no news to write to Wyvil, and he mentally resolved that Wyvil should hear nothing about it.

He would fain have avoided returning to Wingbourne, for he dreaded extremely meeting Mr. Carslope again, and it was with considerable satisfaction that, on arriving there late on the night of his visit to the Fell Cottage, he learned that the master of Wingbourne had been unwell all day, and had not left his room; and he determined to leave the place too early the next morning to run the chance of meeting with any of the family.

But though he had ordered himself to be called early, another had risen earlier still, and when he came down stairs to snatch a traveller's breakfast before starting, he found Florence in the sitting-room waiting for him.

" My dear Miss Carslope, I hope you are better. I had no idea I should have the pleasure of seeing you again before I started."

To this Florence made no reply, but sank into a chair, signing to him impatiently to shut the door. Mr. Crowe complied, her agitated manner showing him plainly that her appearance downstairs was connected with his late mission, and he heartily wished he had never undertaken it at all. It was now too late to flinch from any questions she chose to put to him.

" I heard you and Mr. Ellerslie talking together the day before yesterday," she began, hurriedly, giving, meanwhile, many a fearful glance to the door, " and I heard you remonstrate with him, and try to induce him to be merciful. I have no time to thank you as I should for your kindness to me, but you said you thought he might find it difficult to prove his case against my father. Is it so?"

" My dear Miss Carslope, I am very sorry you should have to enter upon such an unhappy question. Mr. Ellerslie could little have thought when he told the whole painful history to me that you were within hearing."

" I knew it before," said Florence, " and believed it to be worse than it is. Ellerslie let me believe that my father's conduct had been intentional."

" Did Mr. Ellerslie ever assert that to you?" interrupted the lawyer, eagerly. " That would tell very strongly against him."

" I don't know if he ever said it in words —he made me believe it," said Florence, dejectedly; " and now, sir, I ask you,—for I have no one else to ask, and by what you have seen of us here, and what Ellerslie has told you, you know we are most unhappy—is there any hope that he will not be able to fulfil his threats against my father?"

" It is a very painful subject to enter upon."

" I know it," said Florence; " painful and humiliating to me that a stranger should know I can only hate the man I am going to marry. Were it not my only chance I would not ask you, but you gave me hope by what I heard you say—that Ellerslie had not the power he boasted to have."

" I had hopes of it, too, myself at that time," answered Mr. Crowe.

" And not now?"

" None at present. There is not a link missing in Mr. Ellerslie's chain of evidence. He can prove beyond a doubt that your father has not, and never had, a right to the estate, and that you cannot inherit it. He cannot claim compensation for the years he has been kept out of it, because until your cousin's death in August he was not the direct heir, and perhaps, because also he has so long been cognisant of the secret. If you had relations, my dear young lady, or if Mr. Carslope had any independent income of his own to support you, you could, at the sacrifice of this property, be at once free."

" And having no relations or friends, can I do nothing to support myself?" said Florence.

The solicitor shook his head. " It would be a hard life for a young girl like you," he said, compassionately, " even if you had been brought up to it; but without that, and your father also dependent upon you  .  .  ."

"Still it may be done," said Florence; " other girls have maintained themselves and their families. Mr. Crowe, if I have not contemplated this before, it has not been because I shrank from the hardness of the life you speak of.  It should be welcome to me," she added, with a slight tremble in her voice, " rather than its alternative; and now that I know from you that Ellerslie exaggerated the disgrace  .  .  ."

"My dear young lady, the censure which will fall on your father will be still very heavy, and you will naturally suffer from it.

If I might presume to offer you advice, it would be to accept the lot which Heaven seems to have marked out for you. If a few circumstances could be forgotten, it might prove, I think, a very happy one. Though Mr. Ellerslie's conduct has not been exactly straightforward, there can be no doubt that his affection for you is sincere, and . . ."

"Stop! say not another word," cried Florence, rising quickly. "I came to you for advice, not for insult; not to be told that cruelty is a sign of affection. Leave that to Ellerslie, sir, to urge. Though I am alone in the world, without friend or help, I can do something for myself and my father, and I would rather starve than be Ellerslie's wife, after this last proof of his deceit."

Mr. Crowe passed his hand involuntarily across his eyes.

"If it was not for her father," he reflected, " I could find it in my heart to offer the poor child a home with my girls." The thought of Mr. Carslope, however, deterred him, and it was a great relief to him when Nichols opened the door to announce that it was time to start if he wished to meet the coach. Florence paid the messenger no attention— she had withdrawn to the window, her face turned away from Mr. Crowe in proud indifference. The kind-hearted old lawyer could not part from her so. He stepped towards her and took her unwilling hands in his.

"My dear, I wish I could help you. I hoped I could when I left home, but I feel sure that whatever course you take, if you let filial duty guide you to it, heaven will bless you, and make it appear less hard than it seems now. Remember me to your father, and if he wants a friend, I'll be the best I can for him. Good-bye, my dear;" and Mr. Crowe followed Nichols without waiting to hear her reply.

"After all," he thought when he had left

the house many a mile behind him, " she may
be better off than she thinks now. That woman
yesterday said Ellerslie had a kind heart,
and though that is doubtful, it is not likely
he will prove a tyrant to his wife, and if she
does not irritate him by any ill-judged show of
dislike, she may have many years of happy life
before her ; she does not look as if it would be
a long one, though. And now what am I to
say to Wyvil? I can never convince him there
was nothing to be done for her. He will be
coming here, proposing a thousand absurd
schemes, and very likely saddling himself
with a wife and a father-in-law when every
penny he has got will only keep himself from
starving for years to come. Even if she has
the sense to refuse him, it unsettles her mind
again, poor thing. I'll not let Wyvil hear a
word of it. Must write to him, I suppose.
When are they to be married ? middle of next
week; sixth of May, Ellerslie said. Then I
will let my letter arrive in London on the
morning of that day, and that will show the lad

there is no help for it. But it's an infamous affair altogether!" and Mr. Crowe wiped his heated forehead, rubbed his spectacles, and glared around him with a ferocity that was highly mystifying to the remainder of the coach passengers generally.

Left to herself, Florence crept up to her father's room. She felt strong in her new resolve to attempt earning her bread, rather than sell herself to Ellerslie for it, and ignorant as she was of the hard realities of the world with which she meant to battle, it seemed to her no such impracticable feat to work for her father's and her own independence. It seemed more despicable to her to yield to her fate from the fear of starvation than to shield her father from disgrace, and Ellerslie had guessed that such would be her impulse, and had therefore in his compulsory explanation, laid far less stress on Mr. Carslope's pecuniary ruin, than on the infamy that would overwhelm him.

" Sell myself to him for money," she murmured, as the indignant blood flew to her cheeks—"not if my only choice was to beg on the high road."

That she would, in fact, have scarcely any other resource Florence did not consider. Her ignorance utterly disqualified her even for gaining a precarious livelihood by teaching, nor was she sufficiently acquainted with any common womanly handicraft to earn a bare subsistence for herself, even if her father had not been depending upon her exertions. But no thoughts of this crossed her in her new hope of escape from the dread which, for the last few months, had been wasting her life away. She discredited Mr. Crowe's doubts,—a gleam of safety seemed to have been shown her, the darkness was less thick, and it would not be without a struggle that she could sink back to her former despondency.

She heard Ellerslie's step in the hall, and dreading to meet him, darted lightly on to her father's door; tapped softly, and hardly waiting for his invitation, took refuge there. Then, when she had secured the bolt, another fear came upon her—the fear of what she was about now to propose to him, and how her father, who had been hitherto unconscious that she knew his disgrace, would bear to listen to her.

Mr. Carslope had not seen her at all the previous day, sending word that he was too unwell to be disturbed. The truth was he dared not meet her till he had spoken again to Ellerslie, and learned how much was known to him. He was certain of this much only— that Ellerslie knew that his previous marriage destroyed his claim to Wingbourne; and this furnished a clue to many a speech in which his imperious kinsman had seemed to doubt his title, and which Mr. Carslope's uneasy conscience, though he could not suppose the secret to be known, had not permitted him to resent. Through the last twenty years of his life he had been haunted by a chronic remorse for the unrightfulness of his tenure of the estate, and the consciousness that he was thus keeping Godfrey Thurston out of his legal inheritance, had operated fully as much as his attachment to the youth in fixing his resolve that his daughter should marry him, and the loss be thus made good. This scruple had not operated in favour of Ellerslie, who, though heir-at-law, had not Godfrey's natural claim on the estate, and who could not, except by gross injustice, have been installed by the former proprietor as his successor.

He had no idea that Susan Hoppner was still alive,—he knew only that she had lived six months after his second marriage, and he had never dared since to make inquiries after her, or even to arouse suspicion by sending her the promised remittance, for which, after his own money was lost, he must have trenched on his wife's income. He had lingered on, never daring to face the truth, hoping and at last persuading himself that death or some other chance had silenced her for ever.

And now he tormented himself to guess what use Ellerslie would make of his knowledge. Would he, as Mr. Crowe had hinted, use it simply to extort Florence's acquiescence, and accept his inheritance nominally as his wife's dowry? Mr. Carslope hoped that he would, but it seemed too favourable a termination to be likely. And then, on the other hand, how far had Florence been let into the secret? Had she been terrified by obscure menaces into accepting Ellerslie—or did she know the whole, or finally, was her unwillingness an hypothesis formed by Wyvil's jealousy, and communicated by him to Mr. Crowe. He longed to know, but he would not for much have had the explanation from the lips of his own child, and he had already, though it was still early, sent a servant for Ellerslie to beg him to come to him, when Florence entered.

Her step was quicker, her aspect more animated than he had seen it for months, but his heart gave a throb of pain as he saw her come in, and he raised his hand more to ward off her approach than in welcome.

They had, however, one listener that they little counted on. Nichols, who saw his young mistress enter the room with a hurry of step and air which had been foreign to her for so long, conceived that something unusual was going on. His favourite scheme was still, as it had been, her union with Ellerslie, though he had been so far worked on by Mrs. Williams as to hope it would not " break the puir lassie's heart." He prided himself on having in some measure forwarded their engagement by wiling Ellerslie from Llanfydd, and when he saw Florence's unusual agitation, and combined it with the lawyer's solemn farewell to her that morning, Ellerslie's late absence, and Mr. Carslope's sudden illness, he was as much perplexed with fear of change as any monarch could be.

To glide softly into the next room and apply his ear to a place where the rats had gnawed the panelling, and which was at the back of Mr. Carslope's bed in the adjoining room, did not take him long. He gained little at first by his manœuvre, for the voices in the next apartment were low, perhaps purposely suppressed through caution. At last he heard Florence say in an earnest and, as it seemed, intreating tone,

"Father, I've suffered so long, and how suffered you cannot tell. I would not speak to you of it before, but now that we have nothing to fear, but giving up the estate, why may I not be free?"

"Cannot you think better of it, Flo'?" said the invalid's voice, querulously. "Ellerslie will be kind to you. I never knew him injure a dog who trusted him. He'll take care of the place and of you too, child, and hide the whole matter for your sake."

"He would do that for his own sake," cried Florence. "Father, he does not care for me.  He would not give up one acre of the land for me.  He has waited for years, because if he spoke sooner, Godfrey, and not he would reap the advantage.  Oh, father, dear, trust yourself to me.  You shall be, you always have been, my chief care.  Let me work for you.  I am young, and can support you.  Oh! give me your consent to abandon all to Ellerslie.  Say you are content that I should refuse him."

There came no answer that Nichol's expectant ear could catch; then Florence continued passionately,

"I cannot be his! I hate him.  Every time he comes near me I wish I were dead sooner.  Father, I have promised you I will do as you wish, but think again; don't condemn me to a life of such misery, for the sake of this miserable money."

"I condemn you to nothing, Flo'," was the reply given after a pause, and, as it appeared to Nichols, with considerable effort.  "I am a poor old miserable man, not worthy that you should sacrifice your happiness to me. Do as you will, my dear. It is nothing to me whether I live or die. I shall not live many hours after I'm expelled from this house which I have grown to love, and which has been my own for so many years. But go your own way; I've not been such a good father to you that I have a right to ask you to give up your happiness to mine."

"Oh, God help me!" faltered Florence; "father, I can refuse nothing if you ask it of me in this tone."

Nichols started up; it appeared to him he had been eavesdropping long enough, more especially as he heard Ellerslie's step near. He began with alacrity to make some arrangements among the furniture.

"Did Mr. Carslope want me, Nichols?" said Ellerslie, looking in.

"Yes, sir; but Miss Carslope has been

with him some time, and I am not sure if he wants you still.

Ellerslie passed on to the next door and knocked. He had to repeat his summons before any attention was paid him. Then Florence slowly unbolted it. As his eye scanned her face, he saw she was well-nigh exhausted with weeping, and he glanced sharply at Mr. Carslope, to ascertain the cause. That gentleman's pale and disturbed countenance failed to reassure him, and he turned again to Florence, who was leaving the room.

"You spoke to Mr. Crowe this morning," he said, in so low a key that it was heard only by her. "Has anything transpired to make me alter our arrangements for next Tuesday?"

Florence made a quick motion of her hand towards her father. She was unable to speak.

"Ellerslie, come here," called Mr. Carslope, uneasily from the bed. "Tell me, is all safe?"

"Florence can best inform you of that," said Ellerslie, coldly. "If she thinks so, all is safe from me;" but Florence had escaped from the room.

"There's no fear from her," said Mr. Carslope. "She is a better, kinder child than I deserve. But, Ellerslie, come to me. How did you learn this dreadful story?"

"It matters little recapitulating it all," said Ellerslie, impatiently. "I do know it thoroughly—Susan, your wife, and the fever which did not kill her, and the letters she wrote to you. I have known it for years."

"Before Godfrey died?"

"Yes, long before; but I am not going to betray you, Carslope. You need not fear."

"You are sure of that?" said Mr. Carslope, faintly. "True, Wingbourne will be yours as thoroughly if you keep my secret—it will be your secret too, when Flo's your wife. But, Ellerslie, you will be kind to her?"

"Kind to her!" answered Ellerslie, with a somewhat discordant laugh. "Only she herself could doubt it. You need not, Carslope."

"I do not—I do not doubt it in the least," said the invalid, with trembling eagerness, for through all his selfishness, he had some of the feelings of a father; "but Ellerslie," and here he stretched out his shaking hand, "she has been used to more than mere kindness. When I am gone—and I shall not live long—she will have no one but you. Promise me you will be tender to my poor Flo'."

"Whilst I live, I swear to you, I will," said Ellerslie, returning with a firm grasp the pressure of the white, nerveless fingers. "You may fairly trust her to me."

"I do. I must, though she does not love you yet, Ellerslie, but that may come; and as for you," he added, reproachfully, "you love her property more than herself, else why did you keep silence only as long as Godfrey was alive, and the estate could not be yours? That was mercenary."

"And you," said Ellerslie, fiercely, " why did you keep your contemptible secret after Flora Ellerslie was dead, and could no longer be injured by the truth?" Then, recollecting the inutility of anger, he continued, with a forced laugh, " We have both to forgive and forget, Carslope. You, the means I used to secure your daughter; I, your deception of my cousin, Flora Ellerslie. Florence will be the future bond between us. As her father, you shall be mine as well. It was not my fault that Crowe had learned your history; but it will be safe with him. I made myself sure of that as we rode home from Llanfydd."

## CHAPTER X.

### ALMOST FREE!

MR. CROWE had designed that Wyvil should
hear nothing of the Wingbourne affairs until
the morning of the very day of the marriage,
and for that purpose did not despatch his
letter till the last post beforehand; but he
had not duly measured the force of the young
man's impatience. As day after day went
by without bringing the promised intelligence, Wyvil sorely repented that he had

allowed the lawyer instead of himself to set out on the journey of discovery, and chafed against the delay. Mr. Joy had told him the marriage would be in less than three weeks time, and it was fast drawing on.

Mrs. Harrison sympathised with his impatience.

"I cannot think why Mr. Crowe should not write," she said. "Do you suppose his letter could be wrongly directed or mis-sent? He certainly would write if he had any good news to give us."

"He can have none," said Wyvil, despondingly; "and yet, so long as the marriage has not taken place, there is hope."

"Perhaps he has been taken ill," suggested his sister.

"No, his family have heard from him, but he makes no mention of Wingbourne; I believe, Alice, he has never made any attempt to clear the mystery at all, and he is unwilling to write to tell me so. This idea pursues me, and, though in waiting we have lost valuable time, I shall set out to-morrow."

"Oh! no, Antony, not you," said Mrs. Harrison, briskly. "I have never seen your Florence, and I should like to see her. I'll go instead."

"You? My dear Alice, that must not be."

"Yes, and I'll leave the children and the Ayah under your care, and set off by the first coach. I'll send and take a place directly. I have been thinking of the poor child there all alone without a single friend to help her, till I've grown quite pitiful. It will not take me long, and if I find I am not wanted and can be of no use, I will come back again."

Wyvil attempted to dissuade her, but Mrs. Harrison was bent on going. To one just disembarked from a voyage of so many thousand miles, a journey across England seemed a very unimportant affair. It might be that she was animated solely by a wish to serve her brother and Florence, or that she thought all who had hitherto tried to help had been sad bunglers, and she could do better,—but she was determined to go, and Wyvil, though doubtful of her powers, was too grateful to her for her intentions, to refuse her offer. He still meant to accompany her, but this she eagerly protested against.

"My dear brother, if we wanted a brave chevalier to storm the old Manor House and carry her away, *vi et armis*, you might be very useful, but I think I am far more likely to come to an understanding with Florence on my own merits; and as for Mr. Ellerslie—he might refuse us admittance if we went together, but he must, as a gentleman, be civil to me if I come as an unprotected female. Now, don't think that Mr. Crowe and I are in a conspiracy to prevent your ever seeing Florence again, but acknowledge that I am right."

Whether right or wrong, Mrs. Harrison gained her point and set out alone; but her journey was not so smoothly performed as she had hoped: the coach broke down, and two or three other accidents so far delayed her that it was not until Monday, the day before the inauspicious wedding, that she arrived in Marchbury.

Aware from her brother's account that she should find no conveyance at the little village inn if she had herself set down there, she preferred driving the twelve miles from the market town.

It was early in the day when she arrived in the valley round Wingbourne. The old house looked almost pretty in its spring adornment of tender green leaves and bright sunshine, and Mrs. Harrison gazed round her with pleasure as she drove up, thinking that her brother had certainly maligned the place.

"It is not handsome, architecturally," she said, "but he might have been very happy here. Ah! poor fellow, he would have been if things had not been so adverse."

The Marchbury postillion opened the gate, and she drove in.

A strange quiet reigned about the house; the stables were to all appearance deserted, and not a servant was to be seen standing about in the yards,—the shutters in the front of the house were partly closed, but that might be on account of the warm spring sunshine which streamed full upon them. Nevertheless, Mrs. Harrison felt a chill of alarm creeping over her, as she recollected Mr. Joy's report of Florence's shattered health. She ordered the bell to be rung, and, whilst waiting, opened the carriage door and got out, to make her inquiries in person.

"Is Mr. Carslope within? Will you say a lady wants to see him?" she said, eagerly, to the man who opened the door.

"Mr. Carslope, ma'am? You are not aware that my master died last night."

" Died !" exclaimed Mrs. Harrison. " I did not know he was ill—what was the cause ?"

" It was very sudden, I believe, ma'am ; but Mr. Nichols can tell you how it was, if you'll step in."

Mrs. Harrison hastily entered, and Nichols was not long in coming to her.

" I am Mr. Wyvil's sister, just arrived from India," she explained, as he looked at her with a sort of all-questioning, nothing-comprehending complaisance. " I had heard Miss Carslope was ill, not her father. Has it been an accident ?"

" I am not that exactly sure, ma'am," answered Nichols, satisfied that she was a ready adopted friend of the family. " My master was ailing ; he had never been strong lately—not, indeed, since Mr. Thurston's death, but there was nothing more than common the matter with him till a few days since, when he was taken ill suddenly."

" With the illness which has proved fatal ?"

questioned Mrs. Harrison, who observed that he came to an abrupt stop.

" I can't be for saying what the illness was, ma'am. He took to his bed, and he has not been fairly well since. It was the day a gentleman came to the house—a London lawyer. Maybe you know him? he was one of Mr. Antony's friends, Mr. Crowe."

" Mr. Crowe? then he has been here ?"

" Indeed, he has, ma'am," said Nichols, "and it is he who, to my private belief, brought the news, or whatever else it was, that made my master ill; for he has never been right since he went. But, however, he was plucking up heart, and thinking of his daughter's wedding that should have been to-morrow, when the day before yesterday a note was brought for Mr. Ellerslie, and the housekeeper, poor, ignorant creature, had it taken to my master, for, she said, the family was all one. And he must have read it, for I went to the room a few minute later and found him lying on the floor; he had had a stroke of paralysis. The letter was lying by him, but just then Mr. Ellerslie came in, so I know no more about it than yourself, ma'am; and between us we took him up to his own room, but he never caught his speech again— if he had his senses it was more than I ken, and though we sent for the doctor from Marchbury, he could do nought, and it was all over by yesterday afternoon. Whether it was the letter or not that killed him, I cannot say."

" And Miss Carslope—how is she ?"

" I cannot say as yet, ma'am. It's too sudden to tell, but she ought to be prepared for whatever the Lord sends her."

" Has she any one staying with her ?"

" There's no one that I ken of to come and stay," said Nichols, stiffly; " forby it's one of the Thurston cousins, and she'd as lief be alone as with any of that set. There's no relation on the Ellerslie side, or on her father's, as you may have heard, ma'am."

"Yes, I know," said Mrs. Harrison; and the tears rose to her eyes as she pictured the desolate condition of the poor girl. It was not a time to stand much upon ceremony.

"She may like to see me to-morrow," she said. "Tell her I shall not go back to Marchbury, but stop at the inn here, and can come to her whenever she wishes. Let her have my card." She took out her card, and wrote underneath her name, the words, "Antony Wyvil's sister," and gave it into Nichols' hand.

"As she has no friend with her, she may find I can be of some use."

"She's not without friends," said Nichols, resenting this as an imputation cast on the family. "She has the best, I trow, that a woman can want, her husband that is to be, and she has no lack of servants to do her bidding, forby Mrs. Williams and myself. But, however, I'll let her have your card, ma'am."

" Do so," said Mrs. Harrison, and she got into her carriage and drove off, telling the postillion that, instead of returning to Marchbury, she should stay at the public house in the village; and there she established herself, with the ease of an old traveller, and the indifference to personal comforts which her kind heart, now more than ever interested for Florence, prompted.

Few people could indeed feel more desolate than Florence on that first day after her father's death. She had clung to him as the one being whom death, or separation as cruel as death, had left her to love. She had consulted his welfare before her own; she had made his wishes the rule of her life;—till when he was rent away from her, she hardly seemed to have thought, wish, or life, left in her that was not taken too. His very errors and weakness had of late bound them together,—her love for him had much of protection in it; and yet, at the same time, she felt acutely that in him, her sole friend and support was gone, and she was utterly alone, without friend or guard—her only relation the person she most dreaded.

Mrs. Harrison's card, when it was given to her the next morning by Nichols, was the first thing which brought any relief to her. Not that she expected help or advice from her; but the name of Wyvil's sister was a talisman to secure her favour, even had she not been so hopelessly poor of friends.

She eagerly declared she should like her to come; and Ellerslie, who feared the effect of unmitigated grief upon her delicate frame, gladly assented to her request, and despatched a messenger to Mrs. Harrison, begging her to come and take up her residence at the house.

With ready, unobtrusive sympathy, which she knew well how to give, Mrs. Harrison came; her quiet helpfulness to Florence, and gentle manners, winning even Ellerslie's regard, not easily given to one of so close a connection with Wyvil.

For that one week, a sort of peace settled down upon that hitherto wretched household. It was the calm of an enforced quietness, during which no old trains of thought could be carried on, or fresh plans started. The hurry—the agitation of life had paused before the threshold of that darkened chamber, where he who had so long occupied the position, though wrongfully acquired, of Master of Wingbourne, slumbered quietly.

All was for the time in abeyance. Even Ellerslie, who had had no love and some contempt for his relative, felt some pity for his death. The end of all his schemes was so near now, when only Florence and himself were left, that he could afford to pause awhile. The mis-spent useless life, which he had so utterly condemned, had come to a close, and his long cherished animosity faded away into compassion, and he asked himself whether his own had not been as mis-spent, and nearly as useless.

But the week came to an end; the earth closed over the remains of what the one had loved, and the other envied, and the future began again to occupy the minds of the survivors. What was to be done next? The question occurred to Mrs. Harrison, who was anxious to return to her children, yet unwilling to leave Florence till something more definite had been settled for her. It came to Ellerslie also, whose thoughts were once more bent on his marriage. The wedding should be as private as possible, from respect to Mr. Carslope's memory; but there were many reasons why it should not be postponed. The sooner he entered upon his real rights over Wingbourne the better; and as Florence had now no protection left, he was anxious to assume that office.

If it was further delayed, he must return to Llanfydd, and leave her alone in the desolate house, which he had no disposition to do; and the circumstance of Mrs. Harrison being there, lightened considerably the ordeal that a marriage isolated from the assistance of any female friend would have inflicted on this poor child. He was desirous, too, of removing Florence to a warmer climate; and it must be his right as well as his duty to take care of her. There must, he resolved, be no unnecessary delay.

But to Florence the future appeared in hard, cruel outlines. She had roused herself from the apathy into which she had fallen on her father's death, and felt that now, for the first time, she was free. There was no further need of sacrifice. She had been ready to brave the terrors of poverty and disgrace, as far as she was concerned, before, but her father's entreaties had held her back; but now he could not suffer with her sufferings, if she were deprived of her fortune, and the stain of illegitimacy thrown on her birth; and it behoved her to be firm to that

resolve. With her father's death, Ellerslie
had lost his power over her. She dared defy
him now.

But though she knew nothing practically
about poverty, it began to have its terrors for
her. Her future plan of work was as yet
unformed; but she began to be more aware
of all that she was not fitted for far more
than of what she could do. Her scanty education had disqualified her from governess-
ship; and of other alternatives she knew
nothing. She had no money of her own,
and a few old-fashioned jewels of her
mother's, which, though she never used
them, had been in her keeping, she rejected,
fearing that Ellerslie might claim them as
part of the property. The number of things
she must prepare, or emergencies foresee,
appalled her; and her dread of the unknown, made her at times disposed to abandon her last struggle for liberty, and sur-
render herself again to Ellerslie.

In this painful perplexity Mrs. Harrison's

society was of no use to her. Her heart had
been unlocked to her new friend at first because she was Wyvil's sister, but in this new
strait Wyvil could not help her. She had heard
he was struggling with poverty himself, and
to ask his sister for advice seemed like appealing to him for compassion or help which he
was in no condition to bestow. She knew he
had once loved her, but if that love were past,
she could not solicit his pity. So she said nothing to Mrs. Harrison about her future plans,
and her friend, though eager to fulfil her
promise to Antony, and to make the offer of
a home, thought Mr. Carslope's death too
recent to admit of any change, and did not
dream that Ellerslie would so soon disregard
that obstacle in the way of his impatience. She
believed she had plenty of time before her to un-
fold her little plan of action ; for Mrs. Harrison
had a scheme, which as yet she had disclosed
to no one, not feeling sure that Florence or
Antony, or even her own husband far away

in India, would approve of it. So she, too, kept silence for the present, and tried to improve her opportunities, not by laying siege to Florence's confidence, but by gentle, unobtrusive sympathy which could not fail sooner or later to win a return.

She wrote to her brother to tell him what had happened, begging him still to trust all to her, and promising him to let him know if her efforts proved unavailing and Ellerslie seemed likely to win the day.

# CHAPTER XI.

## THE ODD TRICK.

But the necessity for decision came sooner than she expected.   One afternoon, about ten days after her arrival at Wingbourne, she was sitting at work beside Florence, who, with unaccustomed needle, was wearying herself over some sombre articles of her future wardrobe.   Ellerslie, at the further end of the room, was looking over the contents of a large desk, one of Mr. Carslope's ill-arranged receptacles for papers, and the light, but determined rustle of the parchments and papers, as with quick, business-like precision, he assorted, folded, and tied up the various packets, was distinctly audible through the room. Mrs. Harrison had made one or two attempts to talk, but meeting with but little response from Florence, she had desisted, and occasional half-stifled growls from old Syphax, who, lying on the hem of his mistress's dress, was fighting his battles over again in his dreams, formed the sole accompaniment to Ellerslie's busy rustling.

The quiet was broken by the entrance of a servant with a message.

"The man who made the offer for the five colts a month ago, is here again, miss," he said, addressing himself to Florence, "and wishes to know if you have thought of it."

"You must speak to Mr. Ellerslie—he is the master here," said Florence, without raising her head.

There was nothing in this answer to excite surprise. Ellerslie had been for many months the sole business manager at Wingbourne, for Mr. Carslope had delegated everything to him, and had Nichols brought the message he would have appealed without hesitation to him. But a report had spread amongst the other servants, how arisen none of them knew, that Florence was to be in some manner deprived of her rights, and it was a matter of pique, and perhaps of chivalry, for them to defer to her on every possible occasion, and show they still considered her as mistress.

Ellerslie would have thought nothing of her referring the man to him, but her reply was couched in a hard, indifferent tone which struck his ear painfully. He looked intently at her in suspense, as if waiting for something more, but she went on working in silence, and he followed the man out of the room to give his orders, and when they were despatched, hurried back to solve the mystery.

As he came back Florence had just thrown down her work with an impatient sigh of vexation.

"It tires my fingers and eyes so," she said, half apologetically, to the more industrious Mrs. Harrison.

"Then don't do it," said Ellerslie, raising it, and placing it on the table. "Come to me at the window, Florence; I want to talk to you."

"I am tired," she said, disregarding the impatient glance he cast in the direction of Mrs. Harrison, and as she did not seem disposed to move, he leaned over the back of her chair and whispered,

"I suppose George interrupted and troubled you; but why say so harshly and so hardly that I am master here? You know I hold the title only under your good pleasure."

"What I say is the truth," answered Florence, steadily, without troubling herself to sink her voice likewise. "You are the

Master of Wingbourne now, and I, for the short time I remain here, am but a guest."

" Guest or mistress, whichever you choose to style yourself," said Ellerslie, " you know your will shall always be law here.    My authority will be secondary to yours."

" It is time for that painful farce to cease, cousin Ellerslie.    I have no right here, and can have none.    The house and estate are yours, and you may claim them any day."

" You forget we are not alone, Florence, when you speak so."

" I do not forget.    Mrs. Harrison already knows everything.    She had a right to hear all I could tell."

" Her right was her relationship to Antony Wyvil, I suppose," said Ellerslie, frowning.

" Her right was because she was the only friend I had," answered Florence, " because she has always shown me sympathy and kindness."

" If it is so, then, I can speak plainly be-

fore her," said Ellerslie. "Have you forgotten our compact?"

"No, I remember it; you have taken care
I never should forget it," said Florence, with
bitter emphasis. "But that compact was wrung
from me, and I am no more bound to keep
the promise I made then, than if it had been
given under torture. It was torture of the
severest kind, but your power is over now for
ever."

"It is the same as it always was!" said
Ellerslie, unmovedly. "One circumstance
has changed, but my proofs are undeniable."

"You mistake—the whole has changed.
With my poor father's death you have lost the
only power you had over me. It was for his
sake only, I gave the promise. I am now
free, and can defy you."

"I have still the power," said Ellerslie,
emphasising his words slowly and deliber-
ately, "to blight your name with the stain of
illegitimacy, you father's with that of crime,

and to turn you adrift from home and fortune into the strange world."

"And into that hard, strange world will I go sooner than become your victim," said Florence, rising. "I will not stop another day in this house where I have no legal right. I had hoped to stay a short while longer in security, but you drive me away. You have given the last touch to your unkindness, and now you can do no more. You shall no longer be burdened with me. You will never hear from me again."

"And what will you do in the world, Florence, when you have left this shelter?" said Ellerslie, stopping her as she was about to leave the room. "Do you mean to wear out nerve and brain in trying to teach? My poor child, you have too many competitors. Do you mean to become a factory girl in Manchester, or a needle-woman in London, to die by inches, day by day, struggling always, losing ground, and at last losing hope—?"

" I have lost hope for many months, Ellerslie. This is the beginning of a new one for me."

" You don't know the world into which you are hurrying so rashly, Florence. You know nothing of the hard wall of prejudice, against which you will be crushed; of the abyss of want which underlies its hurrying, struggling surface, into which an unaided woman falls. A man cannot make his way always, a woman must fail. You do not know the world which—"

Mrs. Harrison had hitherto listened in silence, though her face had glowed with indignation, as Ellerslie went on, but her womanly sympathies could endure it no longer, and she broke in,

" If Florence does not know the world, I do, Mr. Ellerslie; and I know what it will say of you for leaving your cousin unprotected and destitute."

" I am not arguing with you, madam,'

answered Ellerslie, haughtily. " If you are in Miss Carslope's confidence you are not in mine. This interruption is unneeded."

" I must only just say this," persisted Mrs. Harrison, " that if you drive your cousin away, it will not be to suffer the want of a home. She will have one with me. As long as I have a roof to cover my head she shall share it. Florence, dear," she continued, "I ought to have said this before; I came to Wingbourne on purpose to offer it. If you can be happy with me, come to me. You shall be as dear and as welcome to me as an eldest daughter."

She said this last word advisedly, though sister, would have been the most appropriate to their ages, but Wyvil was so constantly in her thoughts that she dared not trust her tongue. Florence turned to her, and putting her arm round her neck kissed her silently. For a minute the two women clung together, the one asking, the other giving protection.

Ellerslie watched them without speaking;

his face, even to his lips, became very pale,
and he stood irresolute, wondering whether
in fact his last chance of success was gone.

"I was wrong," he said, after a pause, "to
insist upon the terrors of the poverty you
would have to endure; I might have known
that friends would come forward to help you
to bear that. But have you reflected enough
on the injury you will cast on your father's
memory? You, his only child, and he is
dead and no longer able to defend himself?"

"You have exaggerated all this to me,"
said Florence, loosing her hold of her friend.
"You made me believe worse of my father
than he merited. Show me all the proofs you
have, Ellerslie. Let me hear the truth from
you for once. Let me see and speak to the
woman herself, and know how far she was
injured."

"You cannot—none can see her now," said
Ellerslie. "She is dead."

"Dead! and you have never told us."

"Why should I tell you? What difference does it make? Yes, she died, the same day as your father did. It was her last letter to him which caused his seizure. But, Florence, her death makes no difference in my claim. Her evidence was merely corroborative; I have written proofs of all I have asserted, to substantiate my claim."

"Let me see them," said Florence, simply, and Ellerslie left the room in search of the papers.

Mrs. Harrison drew a long breath of relief. "He is worse than I ever thought he could be," she said. "Florence, my poor darling, what must he not have made you suffer!"

"More than I can tell,—more than he thinks. I will do him justice ; I do not think he knows all that he has made me suffer. But it is all over now, thanks to you, dear— dear Alice."

There was no more said till Ellerslie returned, bringing in his hand a small deed box.

" The proofs are here," he said, placing it
on the table, and drawing a chair aside of it
for Florence. He did not address, and
seemed as if he were unconscious of the
presence of, Mrs. Harrison, but placed himself
aside of Florence, unlocked the box, and
took out the papers one by one, making on
each the barest comment sufficient to let her
understand the nature of each document, but
ignoring the extreme personal interest that
both possessed in them.

" Here," he said, " you have the certificate
of marriage, the one Susan Hoppner had
always kept by her—the same names are of
course to be found in the old church registry ;
I looked for them once, and found them.
This is the attestation of a woman who knew
her and nursed her in New York, and this is
the writing of the Captain of the vessel."

Florence said not a word as the various
documents were placed beneath her eye.
When she came to the torn letter, still

crumpled by the fossils it had wrapped up for so many years, she looked with a hasty, questioning glance to Ellerslie.

"I got that by accident," he said. "I did not know its value till long afterwards," and she read on.

"And now," she asked, "where is the last letter she wrote, the one which you say my father saw, and which you believe killed him?"

"Here at the bottom of the box, enclosed in one to me. I ought to tell you, Florence, that I believe he has been ignorant these many years that she was still alive, and that it was the shock of discovering this which caused his attack."

Florence turned over the other papers with a hurried hand. "There is no document you have shown me yet to prove that he really thought her dead at the time he married ?" she said, in a disappointed tone.

"I have nothing to prove that," said Ellerslie. "When you accused me of deceiving you by saying your father had been a conscious agent throughout, I had no facts to show it was not so."

Florence pressed her hand to her eyes. "There is still this letter," said Ellerslie. "Do you care to read it?"

She obeyed mechanically. It was written apparently with painful effort, and at long intervals, as if the writer's strength had failed.

"DEAR SIR,

"It may be that Mr. Ellerslie will give you this letter, although I am writing it without his permission, a thing I would not have done, only that I feel the hand of death is heavy upon me and I have no time to ask his forgiveness for writing to you. He has been, and is, the only friend I have known since I came to England eight years ago, and without his help I must have died long since, so I have reason to be grateful to him.

" Dear Sir,—I will not call you husband, for you refused when you left me, ever to bear that name, and though when I left America I was determined to make you acknowledge me, the time for that has long since gone by. I did not blame you much for leaving me; we both had our faults and things to pass over, for my share of which I am heartily sorry, but you left me amongst strangers, you neglected to send me the support you promised, and when I wrote to you, you left my letters unanswered. I have had a weary struggle to live, and if you were to see me now, I think you would not know me, I am so changed.

"It was a cruel thing to do, and I meant to make you repair it. I did not forgive you, I could not, and I meant to make you acknowledge me as your wife. I should have come to you then if it had not been for my accident, and Mr. Ellerslie has since prevented my writing, saying I should do your family a great injury by it, and get no good.

"And now I write because I am dying, and I do not wish to part in unkindness from you whom I once loved very faithfully. I never could forgive you before, but I do now, and from my heart. I have told no one of my secret except Mr. Ellerslie, the gentleman he brought to see me, and last night the doctor he had sent to me, Mr. Joy, who promised to say nothing. So that if you care about my forgiveness you have it fully, and I am a dying woman and shall never trouble you again, and sign myself, for the last time on this earth, your very faithful wife,

"SUSAN CARSLOPE."

"She must have suffered very much," said Florence, as tears rolled down her cheeks. "Ellerslie, she says you were always kind to her."

"I tried to be, more for my own sake than for hers, poor thing. I only deserved her gratitude really for the first few months."

He put the papers back slowly one by one into the box, in silence. Neither were disposed to break it. Florence was thinking sadly of her father, and of the humble, loving woman, whom in his selfishness, or indolence, he had left to despair, and Ellerslie was too intent on watching her softened, sad look, indicating, he thought possibly, a relenting towards himself, to interrupt her reverie. He closed the box again, but did not lock it.

"I have shown you all faithfully now," he said, at last. "If I exaggerated, it was done with no hard motive—the facts were hard enough of themselves. This poor woman had a painful life, and if I persuaded her against making it better, for my own sake, may heaven forgive me!"

"She says you were kind to her," repeated Florence, in a softer accent than she had hitherto used. "It is something to me to find once again, if but in this, the kind-hearted, generous cousin whom I once knew, and had lost."

Mrs. Harrison was still in the room, but Ellerslie had long since forgotten her presence, and he exclaimed passionately,

" Florence, Florence, if I was hard, cruel, merciless to you, remember what I had at stake—how long I waited, how I tried to win your love, how hopeless I was of any other means before I used this. Think, remember that I had had that secret in my hands for years; that at any rate after August, I had everything to gain by disclosing it; that I was mad with passion for your love, and knew no other way to gain it. If you had given me one word of hope, if you had not told me plainly you loved another, I would have waited still. I hated myself all the time I was making you suffer, but I was desperate and knew no other way."

" No other way, Ellerslie ? Did you think that love was to be won by fear or by threats ?"

" I don't know what I thought. I believed I might win your love in time; I thought

you could not despise my heart if you could
but come to know it. But you would not try,
you would not give me a chance. You professed to feel only cold friendship, and afterwards dislike. Oh! Florence, I know I have
made you miserable; I have seen it. I have
felt whilst you were ill I could die myself to
save you—I could have done everything but
give you up altogether. Be generous and say
you forgive me."

"I will forgive you, Ellerslie, all the pain
and all the anguish you have cost me, when
we part. I cannot do it now—not while I
am still here with you in this house."

"And when you leave," said Ellerslie,
"have you ever thought of what you leave
me to? You say you can forgive me, can
you not pity as well? Think of what my
life has been—a loveless, sunless desert,—I
have hardly known a friend, never known
what it was to have love for my own sake.
I cannot remember my mother, I never had a

sister ; mother, sister, wife, all were denied
me; I never knew any of the sweet home
ties which endear life to other men. I have
never had a home; through life I have been
a wanderer and an alien; seeing what love
was in others, but never knowing it myself—
a long, long, life of poverty and disappointment. I was proud, and I had to struggle—
my loneliness was uncheered by any pleasure.
I do not say I had a right to more than I
possessed, but I had been brought up to think
I had ; and then I discovered this secret, and
knew that there was but one man who stood
between me and what I longed for. He was
advanced to all that I cared for, that I had
envied, love, home, riches, friends—Godfrey
had all. Can you wonder there was no
cousinship between us ? And when I learnt
to value you, the breach between us became
wider. And then you became free, and I
was able once more to hope. I saw everything
which my life long I had longed for, within

my grasp. I thought myself sure of winning you. For the first time I felt compassion for your father, and resolved not to expose him. And then you slipped away from me, never perhaps to come back to me, and I became desperate. I have been cruel to you. I have been within an ace of being a yet deeper villain; but yet, Florence, my first, my only love, will not you pardon me?"

"Oh, Ellerslie," said Florence, with trembling voice, and starting tears, "why did you not speak to me sooner so? It is too late now; I may pity, but I might once have done more. I cannot, cannot, forget all that I have suffered, and I cannot love you now."

"And have I not suffered, too?" said Ellerslie.

Mrs. Harrison had hitherto remained a passive spectator. It was no part of her business to overlook the papers the two had been examining, or to listen to the mutual recrimination which she had expected would follow. Her duty was to protect Florence, but beyond this she had no right to interfere. But Ellerslie's last vehement speech had roused her to attention, and she saw with dismay Florence's glistening eyes and quivering lip, and heard her answer, which, though couched in words of refusal, sounded as if pity and relenting were busy at her heart. Mrs. Harrison thought of Antony, and of his unhappiness if at this last moment, when all seemed drawing to a safe conclusion, she should yield to Ellerslie's persuasions, though not to his threats. Strong in the determination that Florence should not be conquered in an unguarded moment, but should have the advantage of calmer reasoning, she threw down her work, and came forward to their table.

"But Mr. Ellerslie forgets that he need not suffer long," she said. "He tells us himself the estate has been his chief object for the last twenty years, and he has got it now. The

best kindness we can do him, Florence, will
be to leave him to enjoy it as soon as possible,
and without obliging him to bring the matter
before the law, which he has far more reason
to shun than we have."

Ellerslie, when she began to speak, had
frowned at her in indignant surprise, but as
she finished he coloured deeply, and was half
a minute before replying.

" Florence will do me the justice to believe,
madam, that my sole motive in asking for her
hand was not to secure the estate."

" But you said a few minutes since that
you had envied the possessors of the one
since your childhood, and that you only cared
for the other last summer," retorted Mrs.
Harrison.

" Florence, is this your opinion of me?"
cried Ellerslie, turning to her.

Florence hesitated; the current of her pity
had been stopped, as Mrs. Harrison meant it
should be, when she made her sharp attack.

And yet Ellerslie looked so unhappy and, to her eyes, so sincere as he claimed her answer, that she could not find the courage to say what, nevertheless, she really believed, that Wingbourne was far more valued by him than she herself ever should be. Twice she essayed to speak, and each time the words seemed too harsh and unkind, though Mrs. Harrison had now retreated to her work-basket, and contented herself with watching them from a distance.

"Do you think—have you thought," persisted Ellerslie, "that my love for riches and station is greater than my affection for you?"

"There are different kinds of love," said Florence; "yours for me I cannot pretend to understand. I think your wealth will enable you to bear my loss better, and that you will more easily forget me here than if you were still poor and lonely at Llanfydd."

"And that is your opinion of me," said Ellerslie, with profound chagrin.

"It is—it must be; and now let us say good-bye. I shall be gone to-morrow. Indeed, it is better that I should not see you again. Some years hence we may meet when the remembrance of these bitter months has faded out of my memory ; when I can better forgive—no, I do forgive now—but when I shall have forgotten."

"You do not forgive me!" he exclaimed passionately. "You call this forgiveness, when you leave me to solitude and despair. Is it on account of my love that you hate me, Florence? or my manner of urging it? Am I so loathsome to you that you cannot forget my vehemence, that you will not trust to my future penitence,—that you will not believe I can make up to you for all, and more than all, I have made you suffer?"

"I might be so mad as to believe it," said Florence. "I might try to forget your vehemence and my misery ; but, Ellerslie, I never could succeed if I were your wife : the remembrance would be a daily stifling weight on me—that you have been a relentless jailor to me,—that you spoke the voice of doom and not love. You made my duty as a child a torture to me. You had me in your power, and you never flinched—never swerved aside an instant for my prayers. You talk of your love—it was not a human love, such as may be requited,—it was the love of a tiger."

"You cannot forgive me because I misused my power when I had it," said Ellerslie. "I cast it away—I have none. I forgo my claims. Will you love me now for myself?"

"You cannot forego your claims—it is idle to talk of it," said Florence, quietly. "You are the legal possessor of these lands ; I am not. If, indeed, Ellerslie, you are in earnest in wishing to do me a kindness, you will not make public the reasons which make it yours, and which involve my father's memory. Draw up any feigned deed of gift, and I would, oh, so gratefully ! sign it."

" And you think that will compensate me for your loss ! You think I care for the vile stuff !—you believe I cannot forego my claims—claims, which, as they injure me in your opinion, I despise and detest. See here," he continued, recklessly flinging open the deed box, and, snatching out the papers, he tore them violently in pieces; "judge me now in that way, if you dare !"

" Ellerslie ! Ellerslie ! what have you done ! the proofs ?"

" Yes, the proofs," he continued, after a minute's pause, during which his fingers had been busy completing their work of destruction; " the proofs on which rest my claim to Wingbourne; there is now only the lawyer's evidence—second-hand at best ; he can prove nothing. You are mistress again, Florence, and I am a landless, ruined man ; call me mercenary again, if you dare ! Say once again that I cared for the estate and not for you, and it shall be the last falsehood your lying tongue shall utter."

"You are mad," said Florence, trembling with apprehension. "Mad! Do you know what you have done?"

"Undone the work and wishes of a life-time," answered Ellerslie, forcing himself to speak with a desperate calmness; "destroyed what I had kept guarded and sacred for years. Repaired, I will not say a wrong, for none has been committed by me, save at the time when I saw your cousin ride down into the river, and raised neither hand nor voice to warn him. There lies my evidence, and with it the power you dreaded, and which made you hate me; and now I am at your mercy, Florence. Can you forgive?—can you pity the loneliness in which you will leave me, which you would not compassionate when you thought riches would console me?"

"Ellerslie—no, this must not be, indeed," cried Florence, much distressed. "I cannot say yes; I will not accept your gift. Cousin Ellerslie, love is not to be bought even by such frantic generosity as this."

"It is done," said Ellerslie, coldly, and, without casting another glance at the tattered crumpled fragments at his feet, he quitted the room.

For a moment Florence looked at the closing door in speechless dismay, then glanced at Mrs. Harrison, and then, sinking into a chair, she sobbed as bitterly as if her heart were breaking.

# CHAPTER XII.

## HONOURS ARE DIVIDED.

"WELL, it is the first good thing I have known him do," said Mrs. Harrison, as the first excitement of Ellerslie's abrupt departure wore off. "He has not quite a bad heart, after all; he could not in conscience, when he found you were determined not to have him, deprive you of estate, house, money, and everything."

" Send after him," said Florence.    " Call him back!"

" To what purpose, my dear child ?    You cannot say a word different to what you have already said ; you behaved admirably. Why should you distress yourself and him by seeing him again ?    Your lawyer is, in my opinion, the only proper person to send for."

" My lawyer! you do not think me so mean, Alice, as to take advantage of what in his frantic generosity he has done?    I shall restore the whole to him at once."

" Well, in my opinion that would be quite as generous and much more frantic," said Mrs. Harrison.    " He has used the most unjustifiable means to possess himself of those papers; and, after all, why should not your mother's estate be rightfully yours ? Because, by a legal fiction, she was not truly married, are you on that account to be disinherited ? If the law would have made over Wingbourne to Ellerslie, it would, as it seems to me, have done a great injustice, and Ellerslie has refused to profit by it. You are both where you were, and where you always would have been had he possessed the scruples of a gentleman."

"It was nobly, it was generously done," said Florence. "To abandon all! to destroy everything!"

"So it was," said Mrs. Harrison, who could not, in her secret heart, help feeling a little admiration for the action, though she thought it prudent to discountenance a kindred sentiment in her friend, "and therefore I would be far from advising you to take him literally at his word. He has given up, not what is rightfully his, but what the law would have assigned him, and I think you ought to come to an agreement or a compromise. Let him have the house and land, as he likes that, on an advantageous lease."

"Is that all, Alice?"

" Give it to him then,—let that be his share;

he is a farmer. And keep ˉyourself what is the other half, the money your father had laid by."

"And if I divide it, how am I to divide myself for whose sake Ellerslie abandoned the whole?" said Florence, with a sad smile. "I cannot deprive him of all at once, and still less can I give him my love for these title deeds. It is best as it was arranged, Alice. You will give me a home as you promised, and let me go to India with you when you return, and leave poor Ellerslie the enjoyment, it it can be such, of what he has pined for so long."

"And what he has risked his soul to obtain," said Mrs. Harrison, in a fearful whisper. "Did you hear what he said about conniving at Mr. Thurston's death?"

"I did, but I am sure it is false—he nearly lost his own life in trying to save him. Will you ring the bell, dear Alice? I must send after him."

Mrs. Harrison gave a little sigh as her dream for her brother's advantage faded away. For herself she was as magnanimous a woman as existed, but for Antony she could be a little mercenary. "I daresay Mr. Ellerslie is already repenting of what he has done," she said, rather maliciously, as she rang the bell.

Nichols came. " Do you know where Mr. Ellerslie is ?" asked his mistress.

" He ordered his horse, Miss Florence, and has just ridden away," said the old steward, casting a searching, curious look round the room. There was nothing in its appearance to explain the mystery which he felt certain existed. Even the little heap of yellow fragments on the floor near the table told him nothing. They could never betray their secret again.

" Do you know which way he rode ?" said Florence.

" He said he was bound for Llanfydd,

ma'am," said Nichols, "but by the gait he rode he will hardly get there, I think, though there may be a special Providence for such as he. I never knew Mr. Ellerslie start his horse at a gallop before. It is well the new bridge is finished."

Nichols departed, and the two ladies looked at each other in suspense. "Is he gone to Llanfydd, think you?" said Mrs. Harrison.

"I don't know, indeed. He may have done so. Did I seem very harsh, Alice?"

"Indeed you were not," said her friend. "Depend upon it, all is safe, and now, Florence; what you have to do is to send for your lawyer—that is to say if you still decline to take advantage of Ellerslie's tardy justice."

"I do utterly," said Florence. "But I shall not send to Solly, my father's agent. He has always seemed to me unprincipled. I wish I could see Mr. Crowe. Do you know his London address?"

"Better than that. I know where he is now, in Manchester; Antony gave it to me. Write to him there, and he will come to you without delay."

Florence wrote, but two or three days necessarily passed without bringing an answer. She heard that Ellerslie had arrived safely at Llanfydd, from a servant whom she sent to make the inquiry, but from him she heard nothing.

Between her and Mrs. Harrison, there was but little conversation, none as to their future plans. Mrs. Harrison strongly disapproved of what she called the Quixotic intention of giving up the property, but as her own brother, she believed, would be the loser or the gainer, as it should turn out, her tongue was tied. Florence knew she gave no sympathy to her scruples, but her feelings had been too strongly moved to recede. She was determined to restore to Ellerslie what he had thrown away. It was not that she thought the law

a just one which would have assigned her
estate to a distant relation; it was unjust,
framed by the world, which generally con-
trives that the innocent shall suffer for another's
fault; but this matter was in her eyes one of
private justice.  Ellerslie would never have
sacrificed his hopes had he not expected that
by so doing he should have won her.  It had
been his last stake and he had lost the game.
She could not give him what he had played
for, but she could return him the stake.

She was still in this frame of mind when
Mr. Crowe arrived.

"It is a most extraordinary affair," he
said, when he had heard all she had to
tell.  "What do you suppose Mr. Ellerslie
is going to do now?"

Florence shook her head.  "I can't tell,"
she said.

"I ought to vary my question, my dear.
What do you mean to do now?  Restore
him the property, you say.  Have you very

well made up your mind on your reasons for doing so ?"

"It is enough that I do not choose to profit by his momentary thoughtlessness."

"That thoughtlessness is not so great as it seems," said Mr. Crowe, after a little reflection. "I have no doubt that if Mr. Ellerslie chose he might revive the whole question. You see there is still the church register to prove that the marriage took place, and I have little doubt he might find people in America, even after this lapse of time, to prove that she was alive after your father's second marriage. If they could prove only a few days, it would be sufficient for his purpose. Then, too, I saw Susan Hoppner, and this doctor, too, (I must speak to him,) and she told it all very circumstantially."

"You do not suppose Ellerslie thought of this possibility when he destroyed the papers?" said Florence, seeming hurt.

"No, I think he honestly forgot it. Still,

if he were to change his mind, the trouble
might be revived again, and therefore I think
your proposal of some compensation a good
one, Miss Florence.   That is not the reason
why you do it, I know, but you must allow
an old lawyer to look on the question from
all sides.   How much do you mean to offer?"

" All that he gave up," said Florence.   " I
mean simply to take no advantage of the
destruction of those papers."

" That is too much," said Mr. Crowe, "more
than Ellerslie can have any right to expect.
You do not wish to be dependent on your
friends all your life."

" Not to be a burden on them," said
Florence.   " I will be independent, but beyond
that . . ."

" Will you trust it to me to make the best
arrangement?" he interrupted.   " You need
not fear that it will be an unfair one.   If Mr.
Ellerslie knows his own advantage as well as
he has hitherto seemed to do, he may make

very good terms for himself, and I, as you
well know, have your interest at heart. But
speaking of this, in what way do you mean
to give him the property? What colour are
we to put on the transaction? You do not
want it to seem as if he took it by right—we
cannot permit that, without injury to your
father. Is it to appear a free gift on your
part? You are not of age yet."

"Not yet, but I shall be in September.
Can I not wait till then and sign it over?"

"You may change your mind before then,"
said Mr. Crowe.

"I shall not," answered Florence, and no
more was said, but when the good lawyer
was alone with Mrs. Harrison, shortly afterwards, he asked,

"Do you uphold your friend in her decision?
Surely not."

"No, indeed I do not," said Mrs. Harrison.
"I don't think Ellerslie deserves it. But I
do not like to be the one to dissuade her

from it.   You cannot have been my brothers' friend for so long, Mr. Crowe, without knowing that Antony has a very great regard for Miss Carslope."

" And you think him likely to succeed now she can do as she likes?" said Mr. Crowe.

Mrs. Harrison laughed,—a gay, joyous laugh. "I really don't know, Antony does not tell me everything, and I'm not in Florence's confidence," she said. " But things being as they are, you can very well imagine that I don't like to interfere with the way Florence disposes of her property."

" She is not far wrong, either," said Mr. Crowe ; " of course making a handsome reservation for herself.   It would just be possible for Ellerslie to revive the whole affair, but a compromise may make it worth his while to be silent."

" And you are to carry the olive branch to -him ?"

" I suppose I must," said Mr. Crowe, ruefully, "but I'll not take that ride again to Llanfydd, if I can help it. I'll get him to meet me at the inn at Marchbury, if possible; if he will condescend so far as to come half way. We must try to accommodate matters."

"There is some one else in the secret, too, is there not?"

"You are right; Mr. Joy. I must see him before I go."

Mr. Crowe called at the village doctor's modest mansion, and heard from him the story of his attendance upon the late inmate of the Fell Cottage, and how she, unsolicited by him, had let him into the secret of her marriage and her wrongs.

"I do not know when I have been more pained and grieved in my life," he concluded. "I could not have believed it of Mr. Carslope. Truly, the heart of man is deceitful."

"At least, a coward's always is," said Mr. Crowe. "I have no need to ask, for, of course, you do not mean to make public this poor creature's declaration."

"You may be certain I have no wish to make mischief," replied Mr. Joy; "but I believe it to be true. She was on her death-bed."

"It would cause nothing but mischief," said the lawyer. "It would deprive poor Florence Carslope of her mother's property, and leave her destitute."

"At the same time," pursued Mr. Joy, "if I am asked for my evidence, I cannot with-hold it; unwilling as I should be to hurt the daughter of my old friend, I must declare what I believe to be true. The poor woman was dying, and I am certain every word she spoke was correct. I took down some notes of it; of course, if the next heir should ask me for them, I must produce them."

"But he will not," interrupted Mr. Crowe. "He and Miss Carslope are coming to an understanding."

"So I always expected," said Mr. Joy, blandly. "If they had not been engaged to be married, my duty would have been much more painful than it is."

"Your duty, my good sir, is to forget all Mrs. Hoppner told you as fast as possible, and, above all, to destroy those notes," said the perplexed lawyer, and he hurried away to write his letter to Ellerslie, requesting an interview at Marchbury. He was not as speedily answered as Ellerslie's correspondents usually were, a sign that the proposal was distasteful to him; but at last a reply came naming a day when affairs, he said, would oblige him to be at Marchbury, and when he would do himself the pleasure of waiting on Mr. Crowe.

At the appointed hour, Mr. Crowe was waiting in a private parlour at the inn, and a few minutes later Ellerslie made his appearance.

Colder in manner than ever, and interposing an impenetrable barrier of reserve between himself and his interlocutor, he waited for Mr. Crowe to make his communication with an aspect of indifference, which, considering the lively nature of their former conversations, must have been assumed, but which made Mr. Crowe feel, notwithstanding his profession, almost embarrassed.

" It is with much more pleasure than formerly that I meet you, Mr. Ellerslie," he said, with a faint attempt at cordiality ; " foeman worthy of our steel, you know. But now you have of yourself abandoned the somewhat questionable stand-point which you had then claimed, and it becomes far more easy to treat."

" I have no desire whatever to treat—I do not understand you," said Ellerslie, who had, by a slight inclination of his head, acknowledged Mr. Crowe's effort to be genial.

But that gentleman was not to be repelled, and briefly explained Florence's desire to make over the greater part of the estate to the next heir in consideration of his legal claims upon it.

"Those claims can no longer be substantiated," said Ellerslie; "they can never be raised again,—Miss Carslope and her heirs are the rightful possessors of Wingbourne. You will excuse me, if I say I see no grounds whatever for a compromise."

"Then it is not your intention to raise the question of her legal title again in any manner?" said Mr. Crowe.

"I should not have destroyed those documents if it had been," answered Ellerslie, with icy reserve.

"Nevertheless, sir, permit me to observe Miss Carslope will not be satisfied with this answer. She has commissioned me to make you this offer—to transfer over to you the house called Wingbourne, with the lands and tenements appertaining thereto, reserving for herself the personal property which will amount, I should suppose, to an equal amount in value; this is on the condition that all family matters which have come under your cognisance, shall remain between ourselves."

"Then take my answer to Miss Carslope," said Ellerslie. " Herself and her estate are inseparable ; I will not receive the one without the other. The Wingbourne property is not to be divided. When I destroyed the proofs of my title to it, I did not do it with the intention of receiving the half as a gift afterwards."

Mr. Crowe was embarrassed what next to say.

" Miss Carslope will not be satisfied with this answer," he repeated.

" I cannot help that," said Ellerslie. " Will you tell her that some time hence, I shall be glad to explain myself personally to her more fully? She can, however, have little doubt of my meaning now."

" You have hitherto made it tolerably clear,

sir," said the lawyer; " but I confess I am at
a loss now. You will neither accept a part
as a gift, nor are going to revive your claims
on the whole.'

" That is intelligible to my thinking."

" And I am to take this back to Miss Carslope as your ultimate decision ?"

" I am not accustomed to retract what I
have said," replied Ellerslie, with an impatient flash of his eye, which showed his
anger was rising.

" All men have to retract sometimes," said
Mr. Crowe, steadily. " You have done so,
sir—retracted, what I must consider the
greatest mistake of your life, and I honour
you for it. As for my proposal, I hope you
will think better of it. Miss Carslope will
not be staying at Wingbourne; she is leaving
in a few days for Brighton with Mrs. Harrison."

" With Wyvil's sister !" exclaimed Ellerslie,
involuntarily, and, ashamed of the emotion

which he could not suppress, he turned away and walked to the window.

Mr. Crowe continued, as if quite unobservant,

"The old place will therefore be sold, or let to strangers, and I believe Miss Carslope and you, too, would be rather sorry for that."

"You have had my reply, sir," interrupted Ellerslie, "and have done your commission. We had better part. You can write to me at Llanfydd if you have any other communication to make, but on this subject they will be quite unnecessary."

He turned towards the lawyer, and held out his hand. "You have told me some hard truths, Mr. Crowe, but you were bound to do the best you could for your clients. I am not a charitably disposed man, but I can appreciate honest speaking, even when directed against myself. Good-bye, and don't think me uncivil, when I hope I may never have occasion to see you again."

"Has not Mr. Ellerslie returned to Llan-fydd?" said a farmer who formed one of a group at the inn door as Mr. Crowe, a short time afterwards, mounted into his carriage. "I heard some one say to-day that the farm was to be sold."

"He'll hardly find a purchaser," said another. "It will not be worth anyone's while to buy it; I suppose he's tired of the place. They said a while ago he would have Wingbourne, but there seems no truth in it."

A few days afterwards Florence and Mrs. Harrison set off for the sea-side. Florence was loath to quit her old home, but there were too many painful memories clinging round it to render it a safe or healthful dwelling for her. On the point of her imme-diate removal Mrs. Harrison was inexorable —and though the uncertainty whether she might ever return to Wingbourne still further endeared it to Florence, despite its homely ugliness, she would not grieve her friend by delays. Mr. Crowe had brought back the account of his unsuccessful embassy, but yet, he conjectured, and Florence trusted it might prove true, that time and the softening down of his resentment would induce Ellerslie to abate something of his pride, and accept the compromise. This the lawyer was still anxious to effect, not from the considerations which influenced Florence, but because he could not dismiss the fear that the same restless and discontented spirit, restored exactly to its old sphere, might find means to work the same mischief again.

"I have only his word that he will not," he thought, "and that will tell no way in law," and for this reason he encouraged Florence to hope that time and reflection would work changes, and a treaty of peace be entered into.

Brighton was not then connected with London by a railway, yet nevertheless Wyvil, during the course of the ensuing summer, contrived constantly to be there—to the prejudice possibly of his reading, but encouraged by Mrs. Harrison, of whose secret plan her brother's law studies formed no part.

"I have come to the conclusion that it is high time for me to go back to India," said Mrs. Harrison at the end of August. "Edward writes to say that he wants me dreadfully, and I am very well satisfied with the lady I have found for the children to stop with. She is extremely kind, and I ought to go to take care of those who want me most."

"Perhaps so," said Antony, to whom this speech was addressed, and who was sitting with her on a bench overlooking the sea; "but I shall miss you dreadfully, as well as Edward; and Florence—who can want you more than Florence does?"

"Why, indeed," said Mrs. Harrison, bestowing the chief part of her attention upon the needlework over which she was busy; "she would find it very lonely to stay here.

She might stop with Mrs. Ferrand as a boarder, but she would find it very dull. She is obliged to stay here until her birthday, Mr. Crowe thinks, to execute all sorts of deeds on which she has set her heart; but by the end of September we should be ready to start."

" We ? Whom do you mean, Alice ?"

" Why, I have been speaking to her, and reminding her that she had no friends to leave behind, and no home that she cared for, as she will not go back to Wingbourne; and indeed she could not live there alone; and I have been telling her how glad I should be to have her with us and how unwilling I am to part with her, and trying to persuade her to come with me to India."

" You have ?" cried Wyvil, breathlessly, and starting up he faced his sister, eagerly expectant of her answer. " And what did she say ?"

" Neither yes or no. I could not get an

answer from her. She would like to come,
I believe, but—Antony," she continued, letting her work fall unheeded in her lap; " is
there any reason why you should not go back
with us? It will be years before you can do
anything or be anybody at the bar here. Do
throw it up and come back with us."

"You perfidious woman! Is this the end
of all your civilities to Mr. Crowe? My
defection will almost break his heart."

"Ah! and I've been plotting it ever since
I came to England. Why should we not
take you back with us? You like India.
There's your old place, or one just like it,
all ready for you, and I am going to take
Florence, at any rate, with me. The break-
up of associations will do her good."

"Where is Florence?" asked Antony, for
all reply.

" Down there—I see her black dress on the
beach. Antony, before you go to her, tell
me whether you will come with us or not."

" It depends on her answer," said Wyvil, and darting from his sister's side, he made his way down to the beach.

Mrs. Harrison watched him approach the black figure; then accost it. What his words were, or what the answer given, she was much too far off to hear, but in two or three minutes' time she saw Florence's hand clasped confidingly in his, and the two sauntered slowly off together, heedless who might be observing them, and totally forgetful of any and everything but each other.

" Very good," said Mrs. Harrison, as with satisfied smile she folded up her work, " I shall have to write and take three passages in the Hydaspes."

# CHAPTER XIII.

### THE INDIA MAIL.

*From John Crowe, Esq., Solicitor, London, to A. Wyvil, Esq., E.I.C.S., Agra.*

*Sept.* 1837.

DEAR MR. WYVIL,—Although not my usual time for writing, I shall take advantage of the present mail to send you word of certain events, which as they will hereafter prove important to you and Mrs. Wyvil, it seems to me proper I should make you acquainted with. Moreover, though I have not been specially enjoined to inform you of them, I have in no way been forbidden to do so, and as my correspondence with you is well known, I accept it as a hint that my doing so would not be altogether unwelcome.

I have at length seen Mr. Ellerslie, and, stranger still, it was at his own request that I went to Wingbourne to visit him. Of course, had he not written I should never have gone, since his leaving your letters unanswered showed that he was desirous of dropping all intercourse. You wrote, I believe, three times after your return to India without receiving any answer, and I had not even business communication with him after the first year, so that beyond hearing of him through third parties, which enabled me to answer your enquiries, I had no intelligence of him.

A month since, however, I received a letter

from him asking me when I was next at leisure to come to see him at Wingbourne. I was curious to see him for many reasons, and I set aside other engagements, and ten days afterwards was enabled to set off.

The Wingbourne carriage was in waiting for me at Marchbury, and I arrived at the house a little after dark. I could therefore see but little of the place, but what I could distinguish seemed to be in disorder; building and planting were going on, and as the carriage never stopped till we reached the hall door, I supposed that the outer wall was thrown down. I was met at the door by the old steward, Nichols, with many apologies to me for his master's absence. It was the night he said of a large entertainment, given by one of the county magnates, and Mr. Ellerslie was compelled to be there. He begged that I would make myself comfortable, and then asked me, more affectionately than I could have imagined he felt, after Mrs. Wyvil. He said he should have known if anything had happened to her, as his master read all the India news regularly, and he must have heard if anything much amiss had occurred.

I talked with Nichols and questioned him concerning the changes which these six years must have made in everything. The old man himself, though his hair is now quite white, seems as hale and active as he used to be.

" I shall last my master's time," he said to me, " and, it may be, see new faces in the old house, though it will be a different place then to what it has been."

" Is Mr. Ellerslie altering the place then so much ?" I asked.

" Ow, he's just building up here and pulling it down there," said Nichols, discontentedly. " The garden is all brought round the house, and the stables taken off to where the garden was, and trees planted to keep it out of sight, and Mr. Ellerslie goes round the country looking at trees, and choosing stone, and sending for bits of slate here, and handsome foreign woods there, as if the house was his main object in life."

"Indeed!" I said. "I understood that he never cared to stay at the place, but left it to fall into ruin, and spent half his time on the continent."

"Weel, so he did; but that was at first," said Nichols. "He never cared for anything that happened at first. The walls might be damp, and the window panes broken, and the roof let in the rain water at the melting of the snow, and he never gave a thought to it, though he always let me have it set to rights. He used to ride out over the hills all day, with not a creature with him but Miss Florence's dog Syphax, and when the creature grew old and lame, I believe in my soul he shortened his rides so as not to leave him behind. It seemed the only living thing he cared about, and when it died he grieved for it I believe as much as if it had been a Christian. Weel, he was asked to many a grand house, and he went sometimes for the sake of the Ellerslie honour, I would tell him, but he always came back looking worse moped than when he went, and if by chance he had any gentleman staying with him here it was worse than ever."

" And how long is it since he has altered?" said I.

" Since last summer, sir; all at once. It was a bad season here, and there was fever high and low amongst the poor, in the cottages, and the village, and out on the hills, and Mr. Ellerslie maun go into the thick of it. I believe, on my salvation, he did more one way or another, for kill or cure, than the doctors did. He hardly rested night nor day, and then he was ill himself—the first illness, he told me, he had ever had—and no wonder, with the hurrying up and down, and the heat, and worry, and want of rest. Weel, sir, it's after that illness that he's changed, and seems to care about the place, to better it, and make it different. And he'll make it a pretty place, there's no doubt on't, though to my eye I even like it best as it was when the Ellerslie family was the grandest in the county, but I shall not live long to see it as it is; and yet, though I'm an old man, I shall outlive its present master."

"Why?" I asked, anxiously. "Does Mr. Ellerslie complain of being ill? Is there anything to make you think that his life will not be long?"

"Nought, sir; and yet, though he's still a young man as compared to me, I still think I'll outlive him. A man does not go on caring for nothing for so many years if he is to make a long stay of it."

"But he is caring for the house now."

"Oh, aye, but whether it's for himself or not I canna be sure. But it's not for me to be talking, sir. I whiles talk too much, Mr. Ellerslie says; but I've seen things in my time, and heard a many more that if I had let out on, would cause a deal of mischief. It's my maxim, sir, that a good servant should hear as much as he can and say as little as possible."

The next morning, when I came down stairs, I was able to see more clearly the nature of the improvements round the house. The whole array of unsightly farm buildings had been swept away, and in their place a green sward, which the last summer's rains had made almost as even as if it had been several years laid down, stretched away before the windows, and clumps of trees and evergreens, recently planted, and still supported by stakes and wires, gave promise of presenting, in a few more years, a tolerably park-like effect. Near the house, a heap of mortar and some scattered blocks of stone, indicated that other alterations were taking effect, but of what nature I could not see from the window. As I was looking at them Ellerslie joined me.

He looks very much the same as he ever did, and the surmises which Nichols had excited were at once quieted. His step is slower, however, than it used to be, and his manner is less abrupt, smoother, and far more gentle.

"You are looking at my improvements," he said; "I shall be happy to show them to you. Will you spare me a day or two here?"

I told him I could, and together we went over the alterations, and discussed them. I need not detain you with a description of them; suffice it to say that in my opinion they are all for the better. I could discern nothing of the extreme eagerness Nichols described in his interest in them, though I should think he spares neither thought nor trouble about them. When we returned to the house, and I had expressed to him my approval of all he had effected, he said, as if following on the train of his own thoughts, instead of replying to my observation,

"Do you think they are such as Florence will appprove?"

"I don't know," I answered; "very possibly; but if you care for Mrs. Wyvil's judgment, I am surprised you should not send her an account of your plans. Nothing would please her or Mr. Wyvil more than opening a correspondence."

"Yes," he said; "but I am not going to write to them—not, that is to say, perhaps for some years, then only when there is no chance of my being here to receive the answer. I have left three letters of his unanswered till that time comes."

"Have you any anticipation," I asked, looking at him curiously, "that the time you speak of is near at hand?"

"Of my death?" said Ellerslie, with indifference. "No; why do you ask?"

"Because you seemed chiefly disposed to consult another's taste in the laying out of your house, sooner than your own."

"As I consider that I hold it only in trust for my kinswoman, that is very natural."

"But," I said, "I think you are mistaking the matter. There was no mention of trust. Wingbourne is your own. You hold it fairly in your own right."

"Such was not my understanding when I accepted it," said Ellerslie, looking at me with the peculiar scornful smile I have now and then noticed in him. "However, whether it was in trust or not, I am so much older than my cousin that my life would naturally end first, and the estate reverts to her as next of kin. So it matters little whether we call it a gift or a loan."

"A great deal," I said—"you may marry. You are still young."

Ellerslie again smiled—this time more sadly than proudly.

"When I begged you to let me see you here," he said, "it was to provide not against that contingency, but against my death. I wish the estate to be secured to Mrs. Wyvil and her heirs, and I want you to see to it."

"Of course," I said, "if you never should marry, she is your nearest relation."

"Yes; but a rumour of the old story got abroad last summer, through that doting idiot Nichols—who learned it, I believe, of Joy, and her right to inherit might be disputed, after I was dead. I should rise from the grave if I thought the evil I did was not buried in it. I want you to make the will, sir, fast, so that no quibble of law can undo it again."

I again hoped that he was not indisposed. He answered this time impatiently.

"I am as well as I want to be—better. I may live to be grey-haired and old, but last summer I had a warning that life must be ended some time or other, and ought not to find Wingbourne unprepared for its rightful mistress."

Mr. Wyvil, I have no more to say. I took

leave of him the next morning, and the will is now drawn up in Mrs. Wyvil's favour. It guards against the possibility of the next heirs, a Scotch family whom Mr. Ellerslie has never seen, contesting her right to the estate. Of course it is not strictly business-like that I should write this to you, and I should have been silent did I not believe that the drawing up of this will is a sign that Mr. Ellerslie would be glad if the long estrangement between relations were over. I am quite aware that it has continued so long only through his determined silence, and I am equally certain that no effort will be made on his part to break it. Still, I think if you or Mrs. Wyvil wrote again, the letter would not receive the same neglect as before. If you or your wife were returning to England, I should not have written all this, but of that I suppose there is no hope for some years to come, and it might then be too late. However this may be, he has sufficiently confessed to me that his sole consolation for a life misspent, and energy and talents wasted and misapplied, would be to see his cousin once again, what, but for his schemes she would never have ceased to be, the mistress of Wingbourne.

THE END.

T. C. NEWBY, 30, Welbeck Street Cavendish Square, London.

# GABRIEL'S
## WHITE ENAMEL CEMENT,

For decayed and discolored Front Teeth. An invaluable stopping,
and warranted to retain its colour under any circumstances.

———

Price 5s. per Box. Prepared only by

London:

27, HARLEY STREET, CAVENDISH SQUARE, W.,

AND

64, LUDGATE HILL, (4 doors from the Railway Bridge), E.C.
LIVERPOOL: 134, DUKE STREET.

———

### TEETH WITHOUT PAIN.

**Self Adhesive.**      **Without Springs.**

"There are none yet produced to equal the Teeth supplied by
Messrs. Gabriel. Not alone are they better, but they are cheaper."—
*Herald.*

———

Specimens may be seen at the Crystal Palace and Polytechnic
Institution.

———

**Consultation Free.**

# F. J. ACRES,

Having purchased the business of the General Furnishing Company,

## 24 and 25, Baker Street, W.,

INVITES ATTENTION TO HIS

## MAGNIFICENT STOCK OF

# CABINET FURNITURE,

## UPHOLSTERY,

## CARPETS, &C.,

One of the largest and most comprehensive in the Trade, and replete with every requisite in first-class Furniture, at the most Moderate Prices.

---

## ILLUSTRATED CATALOGUES FREE BY POST.

---

# F. J. ACRES,

## 24 AND 25, BAKER STREET, W.

New and Revised Edition. Price 12s.

# THE VOICE AND SINGING,

### (The Formation and Cultivation of the Voice for Singing),

### By ÁDOLFO FERRARI.

"The great and deserved success of this work has brought it, in no long time to a second edition, carefully revised, and enriched with a number of additional exercises, which greatly increase its value.

"Since its first publication this book has met with general acceptance, and is now used as a vade mecum by many of the most eminent and intelligent vocal instructors both in the metropolis and the provinces. We say vocal instructors, because it is only to instructors that works of this class can be of material use. Singing is not an art which can be learned by solitary study with the help of books, and those who are self-taught (as it is called) are always badly taught. But a good treatise, in which the principles and rules of the art, founded on reason and experience, are clearly expressed, is of infinite value, first to instructors. in assisting them to adopt a rational and efficient method of teaching, and next to pupils themselves, in constantly reminding them of, and enabling them to profit by, the lessons of their master. In both these ways Signor Ferrari's works have been found pre-eminently useful.

"The foundation of singing is the formation of the voice. A bad voice cannot be made a good one; but the most mediocre voice may be made a source of pleasure both to its possessor and to others. Accordingly, ample dissertations on the formation of the voice abound in our treatise on singing. But it unfortunately happens that these dissertations are more calculated to perplex than to enlighten the reader. We could refer to well known works by professors of singing of great and fashionable name, in which the rules for the formation of the voice are propounded with such a parade of science, and with descriptions of the vocal organs So minute, and so full of Greek anatomical terms, that no unlearned reader can possibly understand them. Signor Ferrari (as he tells us) was brought up to the medical profession before, following the bent of his inclination, he betook himself to the study of music. But this circumstance, while it made him acquainted with the physical construction of the human organs of sound, has not led him into the common error of displaying superfluous learning. We have not a word about the 'glottis,' or the 'trachæa,' but we have a broad principle distinctly enunciated, and intelligent to everybody.

"Signor Ferrari's principle is of the simplest kind. 'Everyone,' he says, 'who can speak may sing. The only difference between speaking and singing is, that in speaking we *strike* the sound impulsively and immediately leave it, whereas in singing we have to *sustain* the sound with the same form of articulation with which we struck it impulsively.' It is on this principle that Signor Ferrari's practical rules for the formation and cultivation of the voice are based. To give the pupil a sufficient control of the breath for utterance of prolonged sounds—to soften the harshness and increase the strength and equality of the natural tones of the voice, without ever forcing it—these are the objects of the scales and exercises on sustained sounds, which must be practised under the careful superintendence of the teacher, whose assistance Signor Ferrari always holds to be indispensable. * * *"—*Illustrated News.*

---

# KEBLE'S HYMNS.

### Just Published. Price 3s.

The new Swiss tune "St. Gall," harmonised by Mr. G. B. Allen (as sung at All Saints', Trinity, and other Churches,) set to Keble's Morning Hymn, with three other hymns by the same author, set to music by the late Vincent Wallace and Mr. W. Guernsey, are just published, with a portrait of Mr. Keble, and a fac-simile of his Autograph.

London: Duncan Davison & Co., 244, Regent Street, W.

In 3 Vols.

# WONDROUS STRANGE,

By the author of "Common Sense," &c.

"We emphatically note the high tone of pure principle which pervades whatever Mrs. Newby writes."—SATURDAY REVIEW.

"Mrs. Newby has made a tremendous rise up the literary ladder in this new and *moral* sensational novel. The interest is so deep and exciting that we read on without noting time till the early hours of morning, and on arriving at the end of this most fascinating fiction, close the volumes, re-echoing the title—Wondrous Strange!"—EXPRESS.

---

In 2 Vols. 21s.

# A HEART TWICE WON,

By H. L. STEVENSON.

Dedicated (by permission of his daughter) to her cousin the late W. M. Thackeray.

"The characters are limned with a steady pencil, and the colouring dashed in with broad lights"—WORCESTER HERALD.

"A simple story pleasantly told."—BELL'S MESSENGER.

"It will be read with the liveliest interest."—PUBLIC OPINION.

---

In 2 Vols. (In October).

# LOST AT THE WINNING POST,

A NOVEL.

By the Author of "A Heart Twice Won."

---

In 3 Vols. (In November).

# NEW NOBILITY,

A NOVEL.

# TO THE LADIES.

---

In 3 Vols. 31s. 6d.

# THE GAIN OF A LOSS.

## A NOVEL.

### By the Author of "The Last of the Cavaliers."

"The story is well told, and the suspense, the constant change from hope to despair at first, and the final triumph of despair forms a most touching part in this history of a true and faithful love."—OBSERVER.

"The author of 'The Last of the Cavaliers' is known to a numerous body of readers, and this new book, so far from disappointing her friends, will give them additional pleasure and fresh reasons for their admiration of a truly talented writer."—MANCHESTER GUARDIAN.

"An excellent novel, in every way worthy of the reputation of the author of 'The Last of the Cavaliers.' For grace, delicacy, and dramatic skill, we have read few things so good in the novels that have recently been in our hands."—LONDON REVIEW.

"The book is pervaded by an excellent spirit."—ATHENÆUM.

# Mr Newby's New Publications.

30, WELBECK STREET, CAVENDISH SQUARE.

---

In Demy 8vo., price 14s.   (In November).

# HISTORY OF IRISH PERIODICAL LITERATURE,

BY

## RICHARD ROBERT MADDEN, M.R.I A.,

Author of "Travels in the East," "Lives and Times of the United Irishmen," "Travels in Turkey, Egypt, Nubia, and Palestine," "Memoirs and Correspondence of the Countess of Blessington," &c., &c., &c.

This History of Irish Periodical Literature, the result of arduous labour and research for the past five years, is not a mere catalogue of names, dates, and compendious characteristics of newspapers and magazines, gleaned from published lists, or memoranda furnished by literary men; but an original and extensive Treatise, illustrative, as it professes to be, of the origin, scope, progress, and design of newspapers, magazines, and periodical miscellanies of all kinds worthy of notice, that have been published in Ireland from the latter part of the seventeenth, to the middle of the nineteenth century.

The importance of such a work executed with due care, diligence, truthfulness, and impartiality, must be obvious to all by whom reliable knowledge is desired, of contingencies, conjunctures, and controversies on subjects of great pith and moment, that have engaged public attention in Ireland during a period of nearly two centuries.

It abounds with periodical notices of Irish periodical originators, contributors, and editors, remarkable for their position, influence, ability, or eccentricity, of past or recent times.

DEDICATED BY PERMISSION

TO

# SIR MOSES MONTEFIORE, Bart.

---

In October will be published, price 21s., in one handsome volume,
Imperial 8vo.

# A NARATIVE OF A JOURNEY TO MOROCCO,

### BY THE LATE

## THOMAS HODGKIN, M.D., F.R.G.S., &c., &c.

Illustrated (from his Drawings taken on the spot) with Chromo-
Lithographs, in the best style of the Art,

By DAY and SON (Limited).

A universal desire has been exprssse1 by the friends of the late
Dr. Holgkin to possess a memento of one whose friendship was
so valued during life—whose death has been so lamented.

It is well known that in 1863-4 Dr. Hodgkin attended Sir Moses
Montefiore in his Mission to the Emperor of Morocco. The Notes
and Sketches, taken during the progress through a country but
little known, and therefore imperfectly described, must certainly
prove highly interesting. Dr. Hodgkin's descriptions are truthful, therefore valuable for the purpose intended—a lasting memento. To render the Work still more pleasing to a large circle
of readers, it will be enriched with a medallion portrait of the
much-lamented and talented Author, a photograph of the tomb,
and a portrait of Sir Moses Montefiore, to whom (with his kind
permission) the Narrative will be dedicated.

The friends and admirers of Dr. Hodgkin, who order copies
before the 10th of October, will have their names inserted in
the volume.

In 1 Vol. (In the Press).

# THE SPAS,

## OR BELGIUM, GERMANY, SWITZERLAND, FRANCE, AND ITALY,

A Hand-book of the principal Watering Places on the Continent.

By THOMAS MORE MADDEN, M.D., M.R.I.A.,

Author of "Change of Climate in Pursuit of Health," "The Climate of Malaga," &c.

---

In 2 Vols., post 8vo., price 21s. (In November).

# SOME WORKS OF NOBLE NOTE,

## By W. DAVENPORT ADAMS,

Author of "Memorable Battles in English History," "Anecdotal Memoirs of English Princes," &c., &c., &c.

---

In One Vol.    Price 5s.

# THE BRIDE OF ROUGEMONT,

## AND OTHER POEMS.

By HENRY J. VERLANDER, B.A.

Author of "The Vestal," &c.

"Forms a very agreeable addition to the stock of modern poetry."—OBSERVER.

"The scenery and accessories are cleverly painted."—LONDON REVIEW.

"Mr. Verlander's muse is one who loves to dwell on the past, and does it with much success."—SUSSEX ADVERTISER.

In 1 Vol.  Price 12s.

# ON CHANGE OF CLIMATE,

### A GUIDE FOR TRAVELLERS IN PURSUIT OF HEALTH.

#### By THOMAS MORE MADDEN, M.D., M.R.C.S. ENG.

Illustrative of the Advantages of the various localities resorted to by Invalids, for the cure or alleviation of chronic diseases, especially consumption. With Observations on Climate, and its Influences on Health and Disease, the result of extensive personal experience of many Southern Climes.

## SPAIN, PORTUGAL, ALGERIA, MOROCCO, FRANCE, ITALY, THE MEDITERRANEAN ISLANDS, EGYPT, &c.

" Dr. Madden has been to most of the places he describes, and his book contains the advantage of a guide, with the personal experience of a traveller. To persons who have determined that they ought to have change of climate, we can recommend Dr. Madden as a guide."—*Athenæum*.

" It contains much valuable information respecting various favorite places of resort, and is evidently the work of a well-informed physician."—*Lancet*.

" Dr. Madden's book deserves confidence—a most accurate and excellent work."—*Dublin Medical Review*.

" It cannot but be of much service to such persons as propose leaving home in search of recreation, or a more benign atmosphere. The Doctor's observations relate to the favourite haunts of English invalids. He criticises each place *seriatim* in every point of view."—*Reader*.

" We strongly advise all those who are going abroad for health's sake to provide themselves with this book. They will find the author in these pages an agreeable gossiping companion as well as a professional adviser, who anticipates most of their difficulties."—*Dublin Evening Mail*.

" To the medical profession this book will be invaluable, and to those in ill-health it will be even more desirable, for it will be found not merely a guide for change of climate, but a most interesting volume of travel."—*Globe*.

" Dr Madden is better qualified to give an opinion as to the salubrity of the places most frequented by invalids than the majority of writers on the subject."—*Liverpool Albion*.

" There is something, and a great deal too, for almost every reader in this volume, for the physician, for the invalid, for the historian, for the antiquarian, and for the man of letters. Dr. Madden has rendered a necessary service to the profession and to the public upon the subject under notice."—*Dublin Evening Post*.

" Dr. Madden's work is fraught with instruction that must prove useful both to practitioners and patients who study it."—*Sanders' News Letter*.

" Dr. Madden deserves the thanks of all those persons afflicted with that dire disease, consumption—as well as of those who suffer from chronic bronchitis, asthma, &c. It is the best work on change of climate that has ever been presented to the public."—*Daily Post*.

In 2 Volumes, Octavo, price 21s.

# ENGLISH AMERICA IN 1862;

OR

## PICTURES OF CANADIAN PLACES AND PEOPLE.

EXHIBITING OUR COLONIAL POSSESSIONS ON THE AMERICAN CON-
TINENT IN THEIR MORAL, SOCIAL, RELIGIOUS, PHYSICAL,
MILITARY, ECONOMICAL, AND INDUSTRIAL ASPECTS,

### By SAMUEL PHILLIPS DAY,

Special Correspondent in Canada, of the *Morning H ra'd;*

Author of "Down South; or Experiences at the Seat of War in
America," &c., &c.

---

In 1 vol., Post 8vo., Price 10s. 6d.

# HEROIC IYDLS,

AND OTHER POEMS,

### By WALTER SAVAGE LANDOR.

"These Idyls may take their place with those heretofore given
us by Mr. Landor. Judged of simply by their merits, they compel
that rare admiration which we yield only to noble ideals made pal-
pable by true art. As recent works they claim the tribute of our
wonder, no less than of our delight."—*Athenæum.*

"The same classical feeling which has given a harmony even to
the most fanciful of his 'Imaginary Conversations,' and moulded
the thoughts of an English poet in the lines of Greek simplicity
and beauty, is to be found here, as delicately marked as ever. Few
artists of modern times have taken a larger range, or have carried
out a clearly conceived purpose with a steadier hand. When Mr.
Landor is gone, we shall have lost at once the founder, and almost
the only follower of a peculiar and grand school."—*Saturday
Review.*

"Here we recognise the dignified pathos and tranquil beauty
characteristic of the best of his 'Hellenics.'"—*Reader.*

"Mr. Landor's works, stamped, as they are, with the impress
of high and original intellect, will ensure for him a proud position among the master minds of the period"—*Bell's Messenger.*

Passages full of vigorous and tender expression, and containing
sentiments and thoughts in accordance with the former works f
the poet."—*Observer.*

"A book of rare merit, containing many passages of singular
power, grace, and freshness of style, which it would be hard to
match in any modern versifier."—*Morning Herald.*

In 2 vols., Post 8vo., Price 21s.

# ANECDOTAL MEMOIRS OF ENGLISH PRINCES,

### By W. H. DAVENPORT ADAMS.

Author of "Memorable Battles in English History," &c.

"There can be very little doubt of these memoirs being favourably received by the public."—*Observer*.

"Mr. Adams manifests the same tact and discretion which have made his former publications so highly interesting."—*Bell's Messenger*.

"The book will interest the general reader and furnish landmarks for the guidance of the student."—*Morning Post*.

"Mr. Adams has here opened an almost inexhaustible mine of anecdotal wealth. Scattered over the pages of our history anecdotes of the doings of English Princes have hitherto been interesting only, or chiefly, in connection with the era in which the incidents occurred. Mr. Adams has shown that the anecdotes have an interest of their own, apart from their historical connection."—*Morning Herald*.

---

### THE FOURTH EDITION, ILLUSTRATED.

In 1 vol., Post 8vo., Price 7s. 6d.

# A NARRATIVE OF ADVENTURES

## IN FRANCE AND FLANDERS,

#### DURING THE LATE WAR,

### By CAPTAIN EDWARD BOYS,

#### ROYAL NAVY.

"Readers will like this curious narrative, which has all the charm of truthfulness, which few writers, excepting De Foe, could have written half so truthfully; and Captain Boys' interesting and patriotic story is all truth in itself."—*Illustrated Times*.

"Many of the events recorded have long since become matters of history; they are, however, so mixed up with personal adventures simple truth conveyed in a simple form, that we read on with unflagging attention."—*Morning Advertiser*."

"Every youth in Her Majesty's dominions should read these adventures."—*Daily Post*.

In 2 vols., 21s.

# IL PELLEGRINO;

## OR, WANDERINGS AND WONDERINGS,

### By CAPTAIN CLAYTON, F.R.G.S., F.S.A.,

#### Author of "Ubique,"

" To read Captain Clayton's book without hilarity would be impossible to the gloomiest of home-keeping hermits."—*Athenænm.*

" A more lively, racy, rollicking ' pilgrim' than Captain Clayton, it has not been our good fortune to meet for a long time."—*New Monthly* (July).

" The reader is somehow so led on and on by the spirit of the book, that the end is reached almost unawares, and ' Il Pellegrino,' left with a sigh.' "—*Glabe.*

" The work is extremely pleasant, chatty, and agreeable."—*Morning Advertiser.*

" ' Il Pellegrino' displays alternate humour and sensible reflections."—*Court Journal.*

" The author was a most thoughtful reasoner on what he observed."—*Observer.*

" The author is a frank, outspeaking gentleman, and the reader will accompany him in his peregrinations with pleasure, whilst those who are going abroad will thank him for the information he affords, and which serves to prepare them for what they will meet with in their travels."—*News of the World.*

---

Price, 2s. 6d., beautifully illustrated.

# THE HAPPY COTTAGE,

## A TALE OF SUMMER'S SUNSHINE,

### By the Author of "Kate Vernon," "Agnes Waring."

---

In 1 Vol. 7s. 6d.

# ON SEX IN THE WORLD TO COME,

### By the REV. G. HOUGHTON, A.M.

" A peculiar subject; but a subject of great interest; and in this volume is treated in a masterly style. The language is surpassingly good, showing the author to be a learned and thoughtful man."—*New Quarterly Review.*

Second Edition, now ready, in 3 Vols., price 42s.

## THE LITERARY LIFE AND CORRESPONDENCE

OF THE

# COUNTESS OF BLESSINGTON,

By R. MADDEN, Esq., F.R.C.S.-ENG.

Author of "Travels in the East," "Life of Savonarola," &c.

"We may, with perfect truth, affirm that during the last fifty years there has been no book of such peculiar interest to the literary and political world. It has contributions from every person of literary reputation—Byron, Sir E. Bulwer, who contributes an original Poem, James, D'Israeli, Marryatt, Savage Lander, Campbell, L. E. L, the Smiths, Shelley, Jenkyn, Sir W. Gell, Jekyll, &c., &c. ; as well as letters from the most eminent Statesmen and Foreigners of distinction, the Duke of Wellington, Marquis Wellesley, Marquis Douro, Lords Lyndhurst, Brougham, Durham, Abinger, &c."—*Morning Post.*

---

In 1 Vol., post 8vo., price 10s. 6d.

# OUR PLAGUE SPOT.

In connection with our Policy and Usages as regards Women, our Soldiery, and the Indian Empire.

---

In 1 Vol., price 7s. 6d.

# TAORMINA AND OTHER POEMS.

"It is written with a rare mixture of spirit and grace, and bears the marks of a highly cultivated mind, enriched by travel and by classic lore."—*Scotsman.*

---

In 1 vol., price 2s. 6d.

# DRAWING-ROOM CHARADES FOR ACTING,

By C. WARREN ADAMS, Esq.

"A valuable addition to Christmas diversions. It consists of a number of well-constructed scenes for charades."—*Guardian.*

In 1 Vol., post 8vo., plates, price 10s. 6d.

# DEAFNESS AND DISEASES OF THE EAR;

The Fallacies of present treatment exposed and Remedies suggested from the experience of half-a-century,

### By W. WRIGHT, Esq.,

Surgeon Aurist (by Royal Sign Manuel), to Her Majesty, the late Queen Charlotte, &c.

---

In 1 Vol., price 5s.

# FISHES AND FISHING,

### By W. WRIGHT, Esq.

" Anglers will find it worth their while to profit by the author's experience."—*Athenæum*.

"The pages abound in a variety of interesting anecdotes connected with the rod and the line. The work will be found both useful and entertaining to the lovers of the piscatory art."—*Morning Post*.

---

In 1 Vol. £1 1s. Second Edition.

ILLUSTRATED WITH FIFTY-FOUR SUBJECTS BY GEORGE SCHARF, JUNR.

# THE MANNERS AND CUSTOMS OF THE GREEKS.

### By THEODORE PANOFKA, of Berlin.

The *Times* says: "This new publication may be added to a series of works which honorably characterize the present age, infusing a knowledge of things into a branch of learning which too often consisted of a knowledge of mere words, and furnishing the general student with information which was once exclusively confined to the professed archæologist. As a last commendation to this elegant book, let us add that it touches on no point that can exclude it from the hands of youth."

"It will excellently prepare the student for the uses of the vases in the British Museum."—*Spectator*.

"Great pains, fine taste, and large expense are evident. It does infinite credit to the enterprising publisher."—*Literary Gazette*·

In 1 Vol. 14s.

## THE AGE OF PITT AND FOX,

By the Author of "Ireland and its Rulers."

The *Times* says : "We may safely pronounce it to be the best text book that we have yet seen of the age which it professes to describe."

"It is a noble work."—*Quarterly Review.*

"It is a powerful piece of writing."—*Spectator.*

---

In 1 Vol., price 5s.

## KNIGHTS OF THE CROSS,

By MRS. AGAR.

"Nothing can be more appropriate than this little volume, from which the young will learn how their forefathers venerated and fought to preserve those places hallowed by the presence of the Saviour."—GUARDIAN.

"Mrs. Agar has written a book which young and old may read with profit and pleasure."—SUNDAY TIMES.

"It is a work of care and research, which parents may well wish to see in the hands of their children."—LEADER.

"A well written history of the Crusades, pleasant to read and good to look upon."—CRITIC.

---

In 3 Vols., demy 8vo. £2 2s.

## THE HISTORY OF THE PAPAL STATES,

By JOHN MILEY, D.D.,

Author of "Rome under Paganism and the Popes."

"Dr. Miley supports his position with a plentitude and profundity of learning, a force and massive power of reasoning, a perspicuity of logical prowess, and a felicity of illustration rarely met in combined existence amongst historians of any age."—MORNING POST.

"Illustrated by profound learning, deep thought, refined taste, and great sagacity."—DUBLIN REVIEW.

"We have no hesitation in recommending these volumes as characterized by learning, eloquence, and original research."—DAILY NEWS.

In 1 Vol. 10s. 6d.

# A HISTORY OF THE KINGS OF JUDAH.

### By LADY CHATTERTON.

" No Protestant family should be without this excellent work."
—NEW QUARTERLY REVIEW.

———

In 1 Vol., demy 8vo., price 12s.

# THE SPORTSMAN'S FRIEND IN A FROST,

### By HARRY HIEOVER.

" Harry Hieover's practical knowledge and long experience in field sports render his writings ever amusing and instructive. He relates most pleasing anecdotes of flood and field, and is well worthy of study."—THE FIELD.

" There is amusement as well as intelligence in Harry Hicover's book."—ATHENÆUM.

———

In 1 Vol., price 5s.

# THE SPORTING WORLD,

### BY HARRY HIEOVER.

" Reading Harry Hieover's book is like listening lazily and luxuriously after dinner to a quiet, gentlemanlike, clever talker."
—ATHENÆUM.

" It will be perused with pleasure by all who take an interest in the manly games of our fatherland. It ought to be added to every sportsman's library."—SPORTING REVIEW.

———

Fourth Edition. Price 5s.

# THE PROPER CONDITION OF ALL HORSES,

### BY HARRY HIEOVER.

" It should be in the hands of all owners of horses."—BELL'S LIFE.

" A work which every owner of a horse will do well to consult."
—MORNING HERALD.

" Every man who is about purchasing a horse, whether it be hunter, riding-horse, lady's palfry, or cart-horse, will do well to make himself acquainted with the contents of this book."—
SPORTING MAGAZINE.

In 1 Vol., post 8vo., price 5s.

# SPIRITUALISM AND THE AGE WE LIVE IN,

By Mrs. CROWE,

Author of "The Night Side of Nature," "Ghost Stories," &c.

---

In 1 Vol. 10s. 6d.

# SKETCHES FROM NATURE & JOTTINGS FROM BOOKS,

By W. H. C. NATION,

Author of " Cypress Leaves," "Trifles."

" The author treats of a variety of subjects connected with the manners and habits of modern life in a humourous spirit."— LONDON REVIEW.

---

In 1 Vol., 8vo.

# A HISTORY OF THE MODERN MUSIC OF WESTERN EUROPE,

FROM THE FIRST CENTURY OF THE CHRISTIAN ERA TO THE PRESENT DAY,

WITH EXAMPLES AND AN APPENDIX EXPLANATORY OF THE THEORY OF THE ANCIENT GREEK MUSIC,

By G. R. KIESWITTER.

With Notes by R. MULLER.

" Herr Kieswitter writes clearly because he sees clearly."— ATHENÆUM.

---

In 1 Vol. Price 1s. 6d.

# THE FIRST LATIN COURSE,

By Rev. J. ARNOLD.

" For beginners, this Latin Grammar is unequalled."— SCHOLASTIC.

In 1 Vol. 5s. Second Edition.

# THE ROCK OF ROME,

## By the late J. SHERIDAN KNOWLES,

### Author of "Virginia," &c.

" Mr. Knowles appears to be only a believer in his Bible, as he comes forward in this work with an earnestness which all true-hearted men will appreciate."— EXAMINER.

" It is a vivid and eloquent exposure of the lofty pretensions of the Church of Rome."—MORNING HERALD.

" It should be in the libraries of all Protestants."—MORNING POST.

———

In 3 Vols. Price £2 14s.

# A CATHOLIC HISTORY OF ENGLAND,

## BY W. B. MAC CABE, ESQ.

" This work is of great literary value."—TIMES.

" A better book, or more valuable contribution to historical literature, has never been presented to the reading public."— OBSERVER.

" A valuable and extraordinary work."—QUARTERLY REVIEW.

———

Dedicated, by permission, to EARL GRANVILLE, Lord President of the Committee of Council on Education.

Price 2s. plain, and 2s. 6d. gilt edges.

# "OLD SAWS, NEWLY SET."

" Earl Granville's recognition of this little book is a certain guarantee of its usefulness and ability. It will cause delight to thousands of young hearts, as well as give a moral tone to thousands of young minds. As a book for schools, and for families educated at home, we can affirm there have been few books published of greater value."—DAILY POST.

" The efficacy and attractiveness of allegory as a means of illustrating great moral truths have been acknowledged in all ages, and Mr. George Linley's genius has done good service in publishing this 'new version of old fables.' This new setting of old saws is well timed and appropriate. Mr. Linley's view is graceful and melodious, and, while he tells his familiar stories in a gay and easy manner, he takes care to point their moral with a piquancy and precision not to be misunderstood."—MORNING POST.

Fourth Edition. 4s.

# THE BEE-KEEPER'S GUIDE,

### By J. H. PAYNE. Esq.

"The best and most concise treatise on the management of bees."—QUARTERLY REVIEW.

---

In 1 Vol. 5s.

# STEPS ON THE MOUNTAINS.

"This is a step in the right way, and ought to be in the hands of the youth of both sexes." - REVIEW.

"The moral of this graceful and well-constructed little tale is, that Christian influence and good example may have a better effect in doing the good work of reformation than the prison, the treadmill, or either the reformatory."—CRITIC.

"The Steps on the Mountains are traced in a loving spirit. They are earnest exhortations to the sober and religious-minded to undertake the spiritual and temporal improvement of the condition of the destitute of our lanes and alleys. The moral of the tale is well carried out; and the bread which was cast upon the waters is found after many days, to the saving and happiness of all therein concerned."- ATHENÆUM.

---

In 2 Vols. Price 10s.

# SHELLEY AND HIS WRITINGS,

### By C. S. MIDDLETON, Esq.

"Never was there a more perfect specimen of biography.'— WALTER SAVAGE LANDOR, ESQ.

"Mr. Middleton has done good service. He has carefully sifted the sources of information we have mentioned, has made some slight addition, and arranged his materials in proper order and in graceful language. It is the first time the mass of scattered information has been collected, and the ground is therefore cleared for the new generation of readers."—ATHENÆUM.

"The life of the Poet which has just appeared, and which was much required, is written with much beauty of expression and and clearness of purpose. Mr. Middleton's book is a masterly performance."- SOMERSET GAZETTE.

"Mr. Middleton has displayed great ability in following the poet through all the mazes of his life and thoughts. We recommend the work as lively, animated, and interesting. It contains many curious disclosures."- SUNDAY TIMES.

SECOND EDITION.

In 3 Vols.

# AN OLD MAN'S SECRET,

### By Frank Trollope.

"As a picture of English country life, with charming development of character, a highly moral tone, and a story of powerful interest, this novel will take rank with the very best of our English fictions."—Globe.

"The portraiture of Dr. Weatherby would not have been unworthy the pen of Oliver Goldsmith."—Daily Post.

"This novel has pith, vigour, and freshness. The story never flags."—Morning Advertiser.

"There is a very decided originality about this novel. It is due to Mr. Trollope to state that he has worked out the intricacies of an elaborate plot very ingeniously. The author of such a story must undoubtedly possess a large share of imagination, and he has powers of descriptive writing to an equal extent. We leave this novel to bear the public test, confident that it will make its way into the favour of a discriminating public."—Observer.

"Certainly one of the best novels of the present year."—Morning Herald.

"The characters are not only consistent and natural, but really interesting studies of probable personages."—Manchester Guardian.

"It is a book which inculcates a rather good view of society, and may be safely placed in the hands of all classes of readers."—Court Circular.

---

In 2 Vols. 21s.

# SHOT!

### A Novel.

## By F. SHERIDAN.

"The plot is well worked out, and a most interesting tale is involved from it. It is a deeply interesting romance."—Observer.

"We have seldom met with a story told so spiritedly. The heroine's passionate love for Lord Scurdith is delightfully depicted. The poaching gipsy is a capital character, whose daring adventures are told by Mr. Sheridan with suitable *eclat*."—Press.

"The story is well narrated."—Reader.

"Vivid descriptions, clothed in fresh and agreeable language, prove the ability of the writer. Mr. Sheridan succeeds in securing the interest of his readers."—Public Opinion.

In 1 Vol.  10s. 6d.

# ASHTON MORTON,

### A NOVEL.

" Both honest and well meant. Its pages do not contain the faintest suggestion of 'sensationalism.' They breathe throughout an air of genuine, every-day religion."—ATHENÆUM.

"The author has evidently sketched her *dramatis personæ* from life ; her models have been carefully and judiciously chosen. We heartily commend ' Ashton Morton' to the perusal of those who desire to meet in the pages of fiction characters and incidents of every day life. There are many characters in it it will not be easy to forget."—PUBLIC OPINION.

In Three Vols.

# MAGGIE LYNNE,

### By ALTON CLYDE,

### Author of " 'Tried and True," &c.

" There are many characters of interest in the novel, and the various scenes are written with talent."—OBSERVER.

"We can honestly praise this novel."—MANCHESTER GUARDIAN.

"A story of strong character and deep domestic sympathies. No novel reader will be able to lay down these volumes till ' Maggie Lynne' has become Mrs. Paul Dillon. We have not lately taken up a work which is better calculated to wile away a quiet afternoon."—MORNING ADVERTISER.

" Sound in tone, enforcing by precept and example sentiments which are calculated to produce salutary effects on the mind of the young."—BIRMINGHAM ADVERTISER.

" There are few writers of fiction who have trespassed so near to the ' wild and thrilling' incidents of the ' legitimate' novel with the same clever avoidance of what is unreal and inartistic as the author of ' Tried and True,' in his present work ' Maggie Lynne.' Where many have failed, the author of ' Maggie Lynne' has secured a fairly earned triumph. The diction is pure, the characters natural, and the construction of the plot clever ; it is no wonder then that the author has succeeded in making ' Maggie Lynne' at once a charming and entertaining novel."—PUBLIC OPINION.

" The author shows constructive power and much cleverness in the delineation of character, with an easy, agreeable style."—SHARPE'S MAGAZINE.

In 1 Vol. 10s. 6d.

# ADVENTURES OF A SERF'S WIFE

## AMONG THE MINES OF SIBERIA.

" In this volume the reader will find a very graphic and truthful idea of the physical condition of a large portion of Russia and its people."—OBSERVER.

" A better idea of the inner parts of Russia may be derived from reading this single volume than from any works of travel." —LONDON REVIEW.

" The story is of deep interest, while the charming sketches of Russian peasant life are deserving of great praise."—PUBLIC OPINION.

" 'The Serf's Wife' might aspire to be reckoned among works of history."—CHURCH AND STATE REVIEW.

---

In 3 Vols. 31s. 6d.

# THE GAIN OF A LOSS.

## A NOVEL.

### By the Author of " The Last of the Cavaliers."

" The story is well told, and the suspense, the constant change from hope to despair at first, and the final triumph of despair forms a most touching part in this history of a true and faithful love." —OBSERVER.

" The author of ' The Last of the Cavaliers' is known to a numerous body of readers, and this new book, so far from disappointing her friends, will give them additional pleasure and fresh reasons for their admiration of a truly talented writer."— MANCHESTER GUARDIAN.

" An excellent novel, in every way worthy of the reputation of the author of 'The Last of the Cavaliers.' For grace, delicacy, and dramatic skill, we have read few things so good in the novels that have recently been in our hands."—LONDON REVIEW.

" The book is pervaded by an excellent spirit."—ATHENÆUM.

---

In 3 Vols. 31s. 6d.

# A TROUBLED STREAM.

### By the Author of " The Cliffords of Oakley. "

" The story is told with much taste."—BELL'S MESSENGER.

" It is a pretty story."—OBSERVER.

FOURTH EDITION.

In Three Vols.

# COMMON SENSE.

### A NOVEL.

By the Author of "Trodden Down."

" To read common sense in a novel is a very uncommon thing, but to find three volumes of common sense is perfectly surprising; yet such is the case with Mrs. Newby's last work. Every chapter contains an instructive lesson in life, an object set before us to acquire, and the means of obtaining it by the most upright and honourable means. It may with safety be recommended as an admirable novel."—OBSERVER.

" We have read this novel with pleasure It is a healthy, sensible, and interesting story. The title is sober, and scarcely indicates the high order of qualities which are illustrated in the narrative—a story which may be read with profit as well as pleasure."—ATHENÆUM.

" We predicted that 'Kate Kennedy' would be the precursor of still higher achievements, and we have not been disappointed. It can with advantage be put into the hands of the youngest novel reader, who may learn from it that the smallest affairs in life may be regulated by the highest principles."—VICTORIA MAGAZINE.

" The whole tone of the book is healthy, the style is easy, and the language well chosen. The love scenes are far more true to life than the sickly sentimentalities we are often invited to accept as heart effusions. The story is built on one great evil of the present day, the living beyond one's means, and we would particularly call attention to the good feeling which is shown as existing between the different classes of society. The plot is simple and natural. It is one of the best novels of the day, the healthy tone of which will place it on the same shelf with those of Miss Austen."—READER.

---

In 2 Vols. (This Day).

# THE STORY OF NELLY DILLON,

### A Novel.

By the author of " Myself and my Relatives," &c.

---

In 2 Vols. (This Day).

# HETTY GOULDWORTH,

### A NOVEL.

By GEORGE MACAULAY.

In Three Vols.

# ALL ABOUT THE MARSDENS.

## A NOVEL.

"An interesting story told with truly feminine delicacy. It is sure to become popular."—OBSERVER.

"The reader who can appreciate home details, charming development of loving natures, kindly sympathies, and small errors of the head—but not of the heart—will peruse this work from the commencement to the close with pleasure and profit."—BELL'S MESSENGER.

"An interesting tale of pure domestic life, very pleasantly written, is this story of the 'Marsdens.' Life, its aim and ends, are earnestly dealt with, and grave lessons are thus naturally engendered. It is a perfectly moral and well considered story, and will prove safe and pleasant reading for our young people."—COURT CIRCULAR.

"Mrs. Waller writes gracefully and agreeably; her characters are true to nature, and carefully drawn. The story is one eminently suited for young lady readers. Nothing can be purer than the tone and teaching of the story."—SHARPE'S MAGAZINE.

"It presents talent of no common order."—PUBLIC OPINION.

———

In 3 Vols.

# TREASON AT HOME.

## A NOVEL.

"It is somewhat remarkable to open a new novel and to find it possesses so much interest and so many striking qualities as 'Treason at Home.' It is written with great ease and power."—COURT CIRCULAR.

"This is a well written, interesting story, which we can safely recommend. We congratulate the author on her success. Lady Tremyss is a well sketched character, carefully filled in, and the fascination which is intended to surround her is plainly felt by the reader. 'Treason at Home' is a very superior novel."—OBSERVER

"It is a long time since we have met with a work of fiction possessing so much freshness and originality."—COURT JOURNAL.

———

In Three Vols.

# IT MAY BE TRUE.

## A NOVEL.

### By MRS. WOOD.

"A highly interesting novel."—OBSERVER.

"'It may be True' is a novel good enough in all respects to warrant us in recommending our readers to read it. It is clever, spirited, sensible, and interesting, and when powerful writing, or vivid description, or genuine humour is wanted Mrs. Wood is equal to all these occasions."—ATHENÆUM.

In 3 Vols. 31s. 6d.

# THE MAITLANDS.

## A NOVEL.

By the author of "Three Opportunities."

"Each chapter is a homily ; every volume contains a world of good advice. The strictest parent might rejoice to see his daughter poring over its pages."--LONDON REVIEW.

---

In 1 Vol. 10s. 6d.

# UNCLE CLIVE.

## A Novel.

"There is no lack of spirit in this story, and the humourous portions are decidedly good."—ATHENÆUM.
"It will claim more than ordinary attention."—BELL'S MESSENGER.
"It will repay reading."—READER.
"It is decidedly entertaining."—OBSERVER.

---

In 2 Vols. 21s.

# KATE KENNEDY,

By the author of "Common Sense," "Trodden Down," &c.

"There is a freshness in this story which makes the reading of this book a real pleasure. This is one of the few tales that may be put into the hands of the youngest of novel readers with perfect confidence."—VICTORIA MAGAZINE.
"A natural, and let us add an agreeable, surprise will greet the reception of 'Kate Kennedy.' We know of no better mode of describing Mrs. Newby's last effort than by classing it with Miss Mulock's 'Christian's Mistake.' The work is full of that suggestive and pointed conversational writing, which carries the story along."—MANCHESTER GUARDIAN.
"'Kate Kennedy' is worthy of the author of 'Wondrous Strange.' More we cannot say, except that it appears wondrous strange to us that the name of the great unknown should be kept a secret. It is written throughout with good sense, good taste, and good feeling, and abounds in vivid and interesting scenes. The story is admirable, and is put together with unsurpassable art, care, life, and simplicity."—BRIGHTON EXAMINER.

---

In 2 Vols. (In October).

# THE MASTER OF WINGBOURNE,

## A NOVEL.

In 3 Vols.

# WONDROUS STRANGE,

### By the author of "Common Sense," &c.

"We emphatically note the high tone of pure principle which pervades whatever Mrs. Newby writes"—SATURDAY REVIEW.

"Mrs. Newby has made a tremendous rise up the literary ladder in this new and *moral* sensational novel. The interest is so deep and exciting that we read on without noting time till the early hours of morning, and on arriving at the end of this most fascinating fiction, close the volumes, re-echoing the title—Wondrous Strange!"- EXPRESS.

In 2 Vols. 21s.

# A HEART TWICE WON,

### BY H. L. STEVENSON.

Dedicated (by permission of his daughter) to her cousin the late W. M. Thackeray.

"The characters are limned with a steady pencil, and the colouring dashed in with broad lights"—WORCESTER HERALD.

"A simple story pleasantly told."—BELL'S MESSENGER.

"It will be read with the liveliest interest."—PUBLIC OPINION.

In Three Vols. Price 31s. 6d. (Sept. 25th).

# OUR BLUE JACKETS

### AFLOAT AND ASHORE.

### BY C. F. ARMSTRONG,

Author of "The Two Midshipmen," "The Lily of Devon," "The Naval Lieutenant," &c.

In 2 Vols. (In October).

# LOST AT THE WINNING POST,

### A NOVEL.

### By the Author of "A Heart Twice Won."

In 3 Vols. (In November).

# NEW NOBILITY,

### A NOVEL.